CONVINCING THE COWGIRL

Books by Jody Hedlund

Colorado Cowgirls
Committing to the Cowgirl
Cherishing the Cowgirl
Convincing the Cowgirl
Captivated by the Cowgirl
Claiming the Cowgirl: A Novella

Colorado Cowboys
A Cowboy for Keeps
The Heart of a Cowboy
To Tame a Cowboy
Falling for the Cowgirl
The Last Chance Cowboy

Bride Ships Series
A Reluctant Bride
The Runaway Bride
A Bride of Convenience
Almost a Bride

Orphan Train Series
An Awakened Heart: A Novella
With You Always
Together Forever
Searching for You

Fairest Maidens Series
Beholden
Beguiled
Besotted

Lost Princesses Series
Always: Prequel Novella
Evermore
Foremost
Hereafter

Noble Knights Series
The Vow: Prequel Novella
An Uncertain Choice
A Daring Sacrifice
For Love & Honor
A Loyal Heart
A Worthy Rebel

Waters of Time Series
Come Back to Me
Never Leave Me
Stay with Me
Wait for Me

CONVINCING THE COWGIRL

JODY HEDLUND

NORTHERN LIGHTS PRESS

Convincing the Cowgirl
Northern Lights Press
© 2023 by Jody Hedlund
Jody Hedlund Print Edition
ISBN 979-8-9852649-8-2

Jody Hedlund www.jodyhedlund.com

Scripture quotations are taken from the King James Version of the Bible.

This is a work of historical reconstruction; the appearances of certain historical figures are accordingly inevitable. All other characters are products of the author's imagination. Any resemblance to actual events or locales or persons, living or dead, is entirely coincidental.

Cover Design by Roseanna White Designs
Cover images from Shutterstock

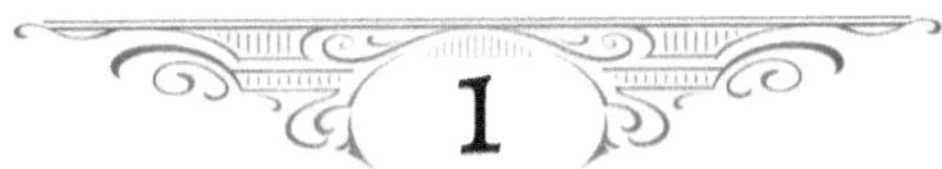

1

Fairplay, Colorado
August 1878

Patience Courtney scrambled to wipe up the stewed tomatoes bubbling over the rim of the pot. But the juice flowed in waves onto the stove, continuing over the side and forming streams on the kitchen floor.

"No, no, no." She had to move the pot off the heat.

She grabbed the handles, but the hot metal seared her fingers. She jerked away but slipped in the tomato and flew backward. In the next instant, her hindquarters met the floor with a jarring thud.

For a stunned moment, she sat unmoving in the middle of the mess. The clatter of the lid and the hiss of moisture hitting the hot stove taunted her, reminding her of all her inadequacies.

Felicity had given her one job. Only one. To move the pot to the backburner when it started to boil.

And she'd failed.

Her scissors lay on the floor near the center worktable, and the slips of petals she'd carefully snipped were scattered over the floor too.

She should have waited to begin her newest decoupage project. At the very least, she should have stopped when she'd finished the sketch. Instead, she'd gotten carried away with the intricate work of cutting the design.

Felicity had warned her. Had told her not to bring any art projects into the kitchen.

Her younger sister knew her all too well—how easily distracted she was and how she lost track of time.

Patience released a sigh—one filled with enough exasperation for both her and Felicity. Was there any way she could get the entire mess cleaned up and everything put back into order before Felicity returned from the emergency trip to town for more salt?

She let her gaze trail over the disaster again before shifting to the high ceiling and large windows. The kitchen had turned into a lovely room. After they'd moved to Fairplay last year, Patience had painted the walls a soft lemon yellow with a crisp white trim. The calico curtains in a cool primary blue matched the blue flecks she'd added to the walls in an attempt to instill a calm, soothing mood like that of a summer day.

After a year and a half of living there, it was finally

feeling like home and less like Uncle John's house.

Patience had been just a baby when Uncle John—her late father's only brother—left the Quaker life behind. He'd gone first to California and then eventually moved to Colorado during the gold rush days.

Uncle John had apparently earned enough from his early mining venture near Leadville to build on the homestead he'd claimed in 1862 as well as purchase surrounding land. Unfortunately, he'd died in a tragic accident two years ago, leaving the homestead to his brother's children—his nieces. To her, Felicity, and Charity.

Shortly after arriving at their new home, they'd realized that life wouldn't be as easy as they'd thought. Although they had the land and home, they'd also inherited their uncle's overdue loans. They'd struggled not only to survive but also to save up and pay off the debt.

Little had they known all that would transpire over the past summer. It had most definitely been a summer to remember, especially for Charity in meeting the man of her dreams, falling in love, and starting a new life with him back in the East.

At a firm rap against the main door in the front room, Patience startled. She peered through the open kitchen door into the dining room that also served as the sitting room. Who was calling?

Perhaps someone was seeking a place to stay. They hadn't had any boarders over the summer. They hadn't needed to maintain their boardinghouse—not after the discovery of gold on their land back in June.

But even now that they were one of the wealthiest families in Colorado, Patience had no intention of turning away a person in need of a place to stay.

Or it could be another solicitor or investor coming to inquire about the new gold mining operation on their property. With the abundance of gold, everyone wanted to take advantage of the riches in one way or another.

Thankfully, Charity had put into place precautions and had hired trustworthy people to run the mine before she'd left for the East. She'd also connected with a reputable solicitor in Fairplay to represent their interests.

They had nothing to worry about.

And so far, after almost two weeks without Charity, Patience and Felicity were getting along just fine. At twenty-one and nineteen, they were old enough to take care of themselves without their older sister.

At least, most of the time . . .

Patience pushed herself up, wincing at the bruise already forming on her tailbone. She wasn't a frail woman, but she was slender and slightly smaller than Charity. While her sisters had inherited their father's fiery red hair and brown eyes, Patience had ended up with their mother's fair coloring—blond hair and blue eyes.

The knock sounded once more, this time louder.

She shuffled forward only to slip, her feet nearly flying out from underneath her again. She quickly latched onto the cupboard that held dishes and silverware, then sidled forward until she was past the soupy mixture. As she exited out of the kitchen into the main room, she wiped her hands on her apron, smudging the linen with not only tomato but also the charcoal still lingering on her fingers from diagramming the design for the decoupage.

Beyond the lacy draperies on the front window, she glimpsed a team and wagon. The back was covered in a tarp but seemed full of boxes and crates and trunks.

When Hudson had been living with them, he'd purchased trunk loads of clothing for Charity and had them delivered to their boardinghouse. Patience smiled at the memory of the day the trunks had arrived and all the oohing and aahing she'd done with Felicity over the exquisite gowns inside.

Having grown up Quaker, they were accustomed to a simpler lifestyle and simpler clothing. She could admit, she'd nearly swooned at the vibrant colors, intricate embellishments, and layers of lace. Each gown had been like a work of art.

Charity had left many of them for her and Felicity. But living in Colorado's high country, what use did she have for such fancy gowns? Not when she had livestock to tend, stalls to muck, a garden to weed, and a dozen other chores every day. Chores that she endured only so that she could finish them and return to whatever art project she had going.

Sometimes she didn't endure the chores as well as she should . . .

Patience brushed at a tomato stain on her blouse, then one on her sleeve. But as the knocking resounded, she swung open the door.

There, standing on the front porch, was a young woman attired in a fine gown—not so lovely as Charity's, but still fashionable, although the neckline dipped rather low and revealed too much of a curvy, voluptuous form. She wore a slight amount of rouge on her cheeks and lips, and her fiery red hair was styled in long ringlets.

She held on to the arm of a man attired in pin-striped trousers and vest with a white coat and matching straw hat. He twisted at his mustache, revealing the dark fingernails of someone used to manual labor, not the leisurely life of a gentleman. The lines and creases in his face gave him an aged appearance—not quite old enough to be the young woman's father, but close.

He'd been eyeing the porch with a critical eye. How could he find fault with anything when she'd worked hard over the past year to create a welcoming atmosphere?

She'd painted a sign in calligraphy—*Courtney Boardinghouse*—that hung next to the door. The windchimes she'd made of colorful glass pieces graced both ends of the wide porch. The window boxes she'd built and painted in bright blue overflowed with the marigolds she'd carefully watered all summer. Other clay flowerpots lined the steps, also painted in blue. Her painted rock creatures—snails, frogs, ladybugs, and more—were strategically situated among the pots.

She'd tried to make the outside as cheerful and bright as the inside. And all of their previous boarders had appreciated her efforts.

"May I help you?" she asked.

"Are you Miss Courtney?" The woman eyed Patience, taking in her disheveled appearance.

Patience crossed her arms in a belated effort to hide some of the stains. "Yes, I'm Patience Courtney."

"I'm Lizette. Your cousin." The young woman spoke in a tone that dared Patience to defy her.

Cousin?

The only cousins she had were in Pennsylvania, belonged to her mother's family, and wanted nothing to do with them anymore. Not after her parents had broken away from the Quaker community.

"I'm sorry." Patience stepped onto the porch, closing the door behind her. Then she studied the woman's face more carefully, trying to place her from among the dozen or more relatives she'd left behind. "I don't recall you. Which of my mother's siblings do you belong to?"

"None." The man's voice was clipped. "Lizette is from

your father's family."

Her father's family? "My father didn't have any nieces or nephews. His only brother, John Courtney, never married and didn't have any children."

"He did marry." Lizette lifted her chin. "And he had me. I'm his daughter."

Uncle John had a child? When? How had it happened? And why had he never told anyone?

Actually, they didn't know much about Uncle John's life after he'd moved away from Pennsylvania. And he hadn't left them any clues in his house, especially why a single fellow had built the two-story clapboard home and furnished it so nicely. If he'd had a wife and child, it made sense that he would have created the place for them.

"I didn't know—we didn't realize—we all thought Uncle John was single until he died." Patience had the distinct impression that she was being rude, that she ought to hug her long-lost cousin, invite her inside, and be more welcoming. But her mind was reeling with all her questions. And one rose to the top of all the others: Why hadn't Uncle John's wife and child lived with him?

"We have proof Lizette is his daughter." The man held up something he'd had tucked under his arm. A large leatherbound book.

"It's John's—my father's—Bible." Lizette exchanged a look with the man.

The man opened the Bible and flipped to a page

marked by a thin satin ribbon. The yellowed page had the word *Marriages* in fancy calligraphy across the top. Cursive handwriting filled the page with the names of couples, all of them Courtneys. She recognized several of the names as belonging to her grandparents and great-grandparents. Her father and mother were listed as well. And the very last entry read: *John Courtney and Wilma Shaw were married October 20, 1858.*

The man pointed to the last entry. "It's right here that he was married. And it's right here that he had a daughter." He moved his dirt-encrusted fingernail to the next page marked with *Births* at the top in the same elegant calligraphy.

Patience skimmed over the page. The names of births in the Courtney family were long and varied. She went right to the end. There, underneath her father, were the names Charity, Patience, and Felicity, each with their dates of birth. Uncle John must have penned them in before adding a final name underneath in neat script: *Lizette Wilma . . . November 10, 1859.*

"Goodness gracious. I didn't know." Patience lifted her gaze again to Lizette, this time taking her in with a growing sense of wonder. She'd only seen a black-and-white daguerreotype of Uncle John in her grandparents' home long ago, so she didn't really remember what he looked like. But she imagined Lizette bore similarities, particularly the red hair.

The man closed the Bible, then dug into his coat pocket. A moment later he produced a stack of what appeared to be letters tied in brown twine. "This is more proof. Letters John and Wilma exchanged after he left his wife in California and moved to Colorado."

The handwriting on the top envelope matched Uncle John's cursive in the Bible. The letter was addressed to Mrs. Wilma Courtney with a California address.

"You only need to read through them to know the truth." The man waved them in front of Patience. "You'll see that Lizette is his legitimate daughter."

Patience wanted to read the letters out of curiosity regarding her Uncle John. But the fellow stuffed the bundle back into his pocket without giving her the opportunity to look at them more closely.

She studied her cousin again and offered a welcoming smile. "The news is unexpected, to be sure. But I believe you."

"Good." Lizette's shoulders seemed to lose some of their stiffness.

"I'm pleased to meet you. I'm Patience—"

"Yes, we know who you are." The man swept his gaze over the yard now. His eyes narrowed as he took in every detail. "We know all about you and your sisters."

"I'm afraid I'm at a disadvantage since I don't know you."

"This is my husband, Gage." Lizette slipped her hand

back into the crook of the man's elbow. "We got married last week."

"I see. Congratulations." What was the age difference between the two? Twenty years? But what did that matter if they were happily married? "Well, welcome. It's a pleasure to meet you both."

Lizette dropped her gaze and fidgeted with a hole in one of her gloves.

Patience waited for her cousin to say something, to indicate what had brought her to the homestead, to express pleasure in seeing her too. But the young woman remained silent.

"The house is smaller than I expected." Gage was now assessing the house—or at least, what was visible from the front porch.

"It's actually quite spacious inside." With three bedrooms upstairs and a small room off the kitchen, she and her sisters had always felt as though they had a large home, even when they'd had boarders.

"It'll do." Gage stepped past her, opened the front door, then walked into the front room. He paused to once again scrutinize the surroundings. Lizette followed him more tentatively.

The two were being rather rude, entering someone else's home without an invitation. Not that Patience wouldn't have invited them in. She was eager to hear more about them and learn what had happened all those years ago with Uncle John and his family. Why hadn't he reunited with his wife and child?

Whatever the case, her cousin and her cousin's husband were here now. And she would do her best to make them feel welcome.

The waft of cooking tomatoes greeted Patience as she stepped inside after Lizette. The stewed tomatoes. They were still simmering on the stove. Probably spilling over the side of the pot even more.

Felicity would strangle her when she returned from town. All her hard work of peeling, seasoning, and smashing the tomatoes would be for nothing if Patience didn't salvage what was left.

Patience started past the couple toward the kitchen. "If you'd like to have a seat, I'll make some tea."

Gage crossed to the sideboard next to the dining room table. "We're not here to socialize."

Patience halted in the kitchen door. "Oh." A strange warning went off inside her. Something wasn't right, but she couldn't put her finger on what it was.

Lizette stood in the middle of the front room and was taking everything in slowly—the furniture, the walls, and even the windows. Were they judging the interior of the home the way they had the outside and finding it lacking?

Gage opened one of the cupboards on the sideboard. He bent to look inside before closing the door and opening the next one.

What was he doing? A guest didn't walk into someone else's home uninvited and start rummaging through cabinets.

"Felicity will be home soon, and I'm sure she'd like to meet you."

"Not necessary." Gage spoke before Lizette could. He snapped the last of the cupboards closed before straightening and facing Patience. "We'll be back tomorrow."

Lizette didn't budge from her spot. Did the color on her cheeks seem to brighten a shade redder?

"Would you like to come for dinner? Felicity is a very good cook—"

"You have twenty-four hours."

"Twenty-four hours for what?"

"To move out."

Patience's heartbeat slowed to a crawl. "I don't understand."

Gage returned to Lizette's side and slipped an arm around her. "We're intending to live here now."

Understanding finally began to make its way through Patience. Lizette was Uncle John's daughter and had more right to the homestead than his nieces. Even so, Lizette and her husband couldn't just show up and expect them to move out in a day. Could they?

Gage nodded, clearly seeing the direction of her thoughts. "As firstborn daughter of the late John

Courtney, Lizette stands in line to inherit everything that belonged to her father."

"Everything?"

"Everything down to the very last fleck of gold dust."

Patience could only stare at her cousin and Gage, cold disbelief winding through her limbs and making her almost numb.

In the blink of an eye, she and Felicity had become homeless and penniless.

2

"Little Miss is without her nursemaid again," the ranch foreman called from a dozen paces down the new fence line where they were installing a roll of barbed wire.

Spencer Wolcott paused in thrusting his shovel deeper into the hard earth. Wiping his sleeve across his brow beneath the brim of his felt hat, he followed the direction Buck was peering.

There, certainly enough, Evangeline was atop her pony, riding toward them across the open range with the naturally growing wheatgrass and brome and bluegrass. The distant mountains on the eastern side of the valley towered above her. At barely four years old, she was tiny even upon her miniature steed. Without a bonnet, her blond hair hung in tangled waves. As unruly and wild as the child herself.

Spencer released an exasperated breath.

At least Evangeline wasn't alone. Tex rode his golden

palomino beside her, his pace matching the pony's. Thank the Lord in heaven above for Tex. Spencer trusted the wiry old cowhand more than any other out of the dozens of men who worked on Trout Creek Ranch.

Even so . . . Spencer's pulse gave a beat of protest. Evangeline shouldn't be out gallivanting across the prairie like a miniature cowboy. She needed to remain at the house where she would be safe and happy, playing with her dolls and other toys.

"She's as cute as a ladybug." Buck grinned from ear to ear as he took in Evangeline's approach. In his mid-twenties, Buck was young for a foreman. But he was sharp, good with the men, and hard-working. That was all that really mattered. "But no doubt about it. She's turning out to be as clever as a coyote."

"I suspect you're right." Spencer braced the shovel against the post.

As Evangeline drew nearer, she nudged her pony to a faster trot. She was delicate and opposite of Spencer in almost every way, from his dark-brown hair to his dark personality. She was the exact image of Honora. Too much so.

Guilt pricked him, as it still often did, even though it had been over two years since Honora had died. What would Evangeline be like if Honora were still alive? His elegant and refined wife would have made sure the little girl behaved like a lady and not a hoodlum.

"I shouldn't have permitted riding lessons until she was older."

Buck snorted, tipping up his hat to reveal his sun-browned face. He was grimy with sweat and dirt like everyone else but still somehow managed to look charming. "Reckon you'd have an easier time keeping the sun from shining."

"Papa!" Evangeline shouted with all the gusto of a ranch hand bellowing out to the steers.

He lifted a hand to acknowledge her call and forced a smile, though it felt tight as usual. Not only had he failed to curtail Evangeline's unruliness, but he was failing her in every other way. He was not a good papa, and he was the first to admit it.

He worked too hard, too long, and too often. But even though he knew that about himself, he couldn't stop. Hadn't been able to stop since the day he'd moved from England to Trout Creek Ranch to oversee the operations for his father. And now that he needed to earn enough to buy out his father's partner, he was working harder than ever to make the ranch successful.

Evangeline hadn't gotten the news yet that he was a failure as a papa. And even now, as she reined in her pony and slid down, she raced the last few steps toward him. She threw herself upon him as she normally did, wrapping her arms around his legs and hugging him.

He patted her back. "Hello, darling."

She lifted her face, giving him a glimpse of the dirt and mire that seemed to cover her more often of late, including the lovely little gown his mother had sent from England. Even so, she was exquisitely beautiful and vivacious and so full of life that his heart ached whenever he was around her.

"Papa." Her blue eyes were the shade of the summer sky above them, again unlike his, which were a green-brown. "I thought I could help you with the fences since you're in a hurry to get them all in place before winter."

Sometimes when she spoke with such eloquence and understanding, he forgot she was so young. And of course, he always had a difficult time saying no to her. But she couldn't help with the fences. She'd only get in the way and end up hurt, likely her flesh torn from the sharp barbs on the wire that his ranch hands called *devil's rope*.

It was a fairly recent invention, and not many of the ranchers in South Park region were using it. In fact, not many approved of his closing in his land. They preferred to have an open range where the cattle could collectively graze without the encumbrance of fencing.

But lately, with the wolves getting so close to the herd, he aspired not only to keep his cattle from wandering off but also to keep danger from creeping in. Additionally, with half of his land devoted to growing alfalfa hay, he had to protect his profit from being eaten up by cattle that weren't his.

Whether the other ranchers were willing to admit it yet or not, fencing was an inevitable part of their future.

He glanced over the sprawling land that went on for close to two thousand acres and to the dozen ranch hands working nearby installing the posts and attaching the wiring in the mostly treeless prairie. The installation of the barbed wire was an ongoing project, one they did when they were between haying or digging more irrigation ditches or calving or branding or any of the other tasks that needed doing every day.

The last haying would begin next week at the beginning of September before they had their first real hard frost. The work would take a week, if not more, from sunup until sundown. And it would require all the hands that could be spared from the cattle.

"Please let me help you, Papa." Evangeline's arms tightened around his legs. "I promise I'll be a very good girl."

Tex hadn't dismounted but waited on his palomino a short distance away. With his hat brim pulled low, the older man's eyes were shadowed. But the rest of his face was visible, a toasted brown beneath the silvery-black beard and facial scruff. Even though he spat a glob of tobacco into the dirt as if he didn't have a care in the world, Spencer could feel the man's urgency and knew he had news to share—news Spencer guessed he wasn't going to like.

"You may as well say it." Spencer pulled himself up to his full height of six feet four inches. After the past two years of heavy labor, his body had turned from sculpted clay into hard steel, and now he had muscles in places he hadn't known existed.

"The nursemaid left." Tex had retained a light accent even though he'd moved from Mexico years ago.

Spencer expelled a sigh even as Evangeline pulled away and bent to retrieve a hammer in the dirt.

His mother had sent him three nursemaids in two years. And in between times, he'd hired reputable American young women. He'd had several from Denver. One had come from Chicago and another from as far away as New York City.

But none had lasted. At least, not more than a month or two.

He couldn't cast all the blame on Evangeline. Yes, she was a handful, to put it mildly. But with the way men outnumbered women in the West, most single women were snatched up quicker than the flick of a riding whip. If it wasn't a ranch hand wooing away his nursemaids, it was a fellow from town.

"Apparently the rise in wages didn't tempt her enough to stay."

Tex cocked his head toward Evangeline, who was now banging the hammer against the post, her cute face scrunched up in concentration. "Little Miss put on a big old show."

Ah, yes, Evangeline could put on quite the show, crying and kicking her legs and even screaming a bit. The tantrums were enough to scare away even the rowdiest and roughest of cowboys.

"Evangeline." He spoke sternly.

She flicked a glance his way but didn't stop her pounding. "Yes, Papa?"

"I'm disappointed to hear that you misbehaved for your nursemaid."

"She told me I was a spoiled and naughty little girl."

And the poor woman was probably right. "Regardless, you must treat your elders with respect, and that includes your nursemaids."

"She said it's time for me to have a mama instead of a nursemaid."

"A mama." The word barreled into Spencer, nearly throwing him back a step.

"Yup." Tex let another glob of juice fly. "Said the only woman who'd have any reason to stay is a wife."

"A wife?" That word hit him even harder.

Tex tipped up the brim of his hat, and this time his dark eyes bored into Spencer. "Reckon it's past time."

Buck whistled. "Ain't that the truth."

Some of the nearby ranch hands guffawed.

Spencer palmed the back of his neck, damp with sweat and grit. And he clamped his mouth shut to keep from saying something he'd regret to the people who cared about him the most.

Marriage had been—and still was—the farthest thing from his mind. He'd had his fill with Honora and didn't want to get involved in another relationship. One heartache had been enough.

"I'd like a mama." Evangeline stopped hammering, and her little face filled with earnestness. "Can I have a mama?"

She sounded as though she were pleading for a puppy. Clearly the child had no idea what she was asking for and how it would change her life. And his.

"Please, Papa?" Her rounded eyes fixed on him with such longing that he couldn't find the words to deny her.

Was it time to get remarried? If not for himself, then at least for Evangeline? Maybe a steady female's presence would tame Evangeline, give her an example of what it was like to be a woman amid so many men.

As she placed the hammer down, he glimpsed her dirty hands, overlong fingernails, and scratches from only heaven knew where—likely from one of the barn cats that she tried to hold every chance she got.

He rubbed at the tense muscle in the back of his neck again. "Perhaps I shall write to my father and mother about the matter."

Old enough to be his father, Tex shook his head, one of the few men on the ranch who wasn't afraid to contradict him. "Mr. Wolcott, boss. You don't got time for a fancy lady to sail across the sea to marry you."

True. And he also had no desire to marry another *fancy lady* of his parents' choosing. Yes, they would find someone from among the landed gentry, maybe even a noblewoman. But after living in the rugged West where class boundaries held little sway, he was coming to the conclusion that a woman's character was more important than her family's status and wealth.

"You've got to marry someone soon. Maybe even tomorrow."

"I see no reason to rush into anything."

"I see it." Tex cocked his head toward the east and the alfalfa. "And it's called a hayfield. What you gonna do with Little Miss during haying without a woman around to watch her?"

Spencer narrowed his eyes at the man.

He held up his hands. "No way, no how. I'm no nursemaid."

Evangeline watched Tex solemnly and then turned her enchanting eyes upon Spencer. "If I have a mama, she can take care of me while you're working, Papa."

Spencer couldn't look at the little girl or he'd give in to her. He shifted his gaze to the alfalfa, a light green with buds of purple but no flowers yet—the sign that it was ready to be harvested at its highest quality for the cattle. He'd learned that once the hay started to blossom, it became stiffer, less leafy, and the quality decreased.

Everyone was staring at him. Even the ranch hands working the fences had ceased their labor to listen to the conversation about his taking a wife.

As though recognizing the same, Tex lowered his voice. "Plenty of men get married to provide a mother to their children."

Of course they did. But why him? Why did the nursemaid have to leave today of all days, so close to the harvest? He didn't have nearly enough time to send a telegram to his friend in Denver and ask for help again in hiring another woman.

And he'd already exhausted the local pool of women. Most were too occupied with their families or businesses to be able to drive out to the ranch every day to watch Evangeline. Even the single ladies, like his neighbors to the north, the Courtney sisters, were too busy managing their own places to take on the care of a little girl.

He held out a hand to Evangeline. "Come, darling. I'll ride with you back to the house." He had no other option but to take care of his daughter at the moment. He couldn't push off his parenting upon Tex or Buck or any of the other men who worked on the ranch. It wouldn't be fair to them and certainly not ideal for Evangeline.

He helped Evangeline back onto her pony and then mounted his gelding and rode next to her. She kept a steady stream of chatter as always, making his job as Papa easy with answers like "I see" and "That's interesting."

Tex rode behind them, and when they passed the large vegetable gardens that provided food for the many workers living on the ranch, Spencer let his horse fall into step with Tex's. Ahead, they neared the two large barns that housed livestock and provided storage for a portion of the hay that didn't go to market. Several bunkhouses and a dining hall had been built beyond the barns to replace the original log cabins that had been there when Spencer had taken over the management.

The main house sat among a grove of oaks and willows near a small stream that wound through the property. The home certainly couldn't begin to compare to the manors his father owned in Norwich and London, the old estates that had existed for hundreds of years.

But the simple white two-story home had become a refuge nonetheless. The front porch was covered and had a swing that Evangeline loved to sit in. And with just the two of them living there with a nursemaid, they hadn't needed anything bigger.

As Evangeline directed her pony toward the horse barn, Spencer reined in. "Maybe I should ride into town and make inquiries regarding a nursemaid. I'll need to line someone up soon."

Tex halted too, his dark eyes taking in the ranch yard, still mostly deserted at the late-afternoon hour. "Heard some news that might be helpful to you."

Could anything truly help him at this point? Maybe it was finally time to consider his mother's offer to have Evangeline live with her. But what kind of life would his daughter have back in Norwich? The rumors of all that had happened with Honora would affect Evangeline and likely tarnish her.

No, the truth was, she was freer here in America, far away from Honora's scandal. Besides, as difficult as it was for him to be a papa, he loved Evangeline and couldn't fathom the emptiness of his life without her in it.

"Very well." Spencer wiped a neckerchief against his face. "What is it?"

"When I was in town earlier this afternoon, I learned that John Courtney had a daughter. She showed up today and is claiming that the homestead and all John's gold belongs to her."

Spencer quirked a brow. "How convenient of her to come home now."

"Apparently she's given Patience and Felicity until tomorrow at noon to move off the homestead."

"She sounds like a sweet girl."

"She's already involved the solicitor and has all the rights as John's daughter, and they have none."

Spencer didn't know much about the Courtney women, but he did know their older sister Charity had married one of the wealthiest men in the country. Surely they would be fine. "And what exactly does all this have to do with me?"

"They have no place to go. Now would be a good opportunity to propose marriage to one of them."

Spencer released a scoffing laugh, but at the sight of Tex's frown, he abruptly stopped. "You cannot be serious."

"Why can't I be?"

Spencer sifted through all the reasons why marrying one of the Courtney women was ludicrous. But they were the same excuses he'd always had. Cowardly excuses that put his needs above Evangeline's. And it was time he stopped doing that. If his daughter needed a mother, then he had to get married for her sake.

Tex's gaze bored into him with a seriousness that reminded Spencer of the gravity of his situation. "The Courtney sisters are well respected among the community."

Yes, they were known for their kindness and generosity. And they were young and exceptionally beautiful. The middle one with the blond hair and delicate features was entirely too pretty. In fact, he was embarrassed to admit that he'd had to force himself not to stare at her on several occasions when he'd seen her around town. The youngest sister with red hair was pretty too, but she'd never caught his attention.

Regardless, he couldn't marry one of them. Could he?

His sights strayed to Evangeline. In the process of

dismounting near the barn in a very unladylike fashion, she puffed out her cheeks, and then she released a wad of spittle, shooting it several feet, almost as well as one of the cowboys.

"Zeus." His daughter was turning into more than a hoodlum. She was becoming a savage. And it was past time to put a stop to it.

"Go over to the Courtneys' place right now, Mr. Wolcott, boss." Tex was watching Evangeline too, his features scrunched with consternation. "If you wait, other men are gonna marry them first."

Tex wasn't wrong. Once word of their plight spread, the women would likely have a dozen proposals of marriage before noon tomorrow.

"I'll keep an eye on Little Miss while you're gone."

Could he really ride over? Tonight? And if he did, what would happen?

Of course, he wouldn't consider proposing to the beautiful blond. He didn't need the constant reminders of his late wife, preferred to marry someone entirely different . . . like someone with red hair.

Spencer nodded, a new sense of determination rising within him. He'd ask the younger sister to be the newest nursemaid. And if that didn't work, he'd propose marriage to her. For Evangeline only. Not for himself. Most certainly not for himself.

3

Patience stuffed the last of her art supplies in the trunk already loaded into the wagon bed. Then she swiped the tears from her cheek.

"I'm sorry, Charity." The whisper escaped into the warm, stale air of the barn.

The silence seemed to condemn her, broken only by the cluck of the chickens in their nearby pen.

The slant of sunlight coming in through a high, round window told her that evening would soon be upon them, and she and Felicity were not one step closer to figuring out what to do.

"I never meant for this to happen," she whispered, as if her confession would somehow ease her guilt. Guilt that she hadn't been able to prevent the loss of the homestead. Guilt that she hadn't yet come up with a way to provide for her and Felicity. Guilt that they had nothing to tide them over until she could communicate with Charity and Hudson.

If only she'd saved the spending cash they'd kept stashed in a kitchen crock instead of purchasing more lacquer and paints and colorful paper. And if only she hadn't used up the egg money earlier in the week to buy the botanical magazine for her newest project.

She hadn't once stopped to think that would be the last of their funds. Hadn't thought they'd need to scrimp and worry anymore.

Now they didn't have a cent, not even enough to stay in one of the hotels in town. Of course, she could turn to friends temporarily. The people of Fairplay were kind and would do whatever they could to help her and Felicity.

In fact, Astrid Steele, their first boarder last year, had told Felicity that they were more than welcome to stay with her and Dr. Steele in their big house in Fairplay. But since Astrid was expecting a baby any day, they didn't want to impose.

Patience didn't want to impose on anyone. More than that, she wanted to prove to Charity it hadn't been a mistake to leave the two of them behind. Her older sister had been worried when she'd left. And Patience had reassured her that she'd take care of Felicity just fine.

Now she had to find a way to do that.

Closing the lid on the trunk, she smoothed a hand over the scuffed wood that had lost its varnish long ago, and she lifted a silent petition heavenward. It wasn't the first prayer and wouldn't be the last. In fact, all afternoon she'd been praying for an answer to their dilemma.

Of course, she didn't want to deny Lizette the right to her father's home and wealth. The young woman deserved to have everything. And Patience hoped her cousin would find as much peace and contentment on the homestead as they had.

Even so, she didn't understand why Lizette and Gage were being so callous and unkind. Surely Lizette could have some compassion for her cousins—allow them more time to get their affairs in order and find a new place to live, let them take some of the belongings that were most meaningful to them, give them some money to help them on their way.

But Gage had been adamant earlier that she and Felicity weren't to take anything from the house except the clothing they'd brought with them from Pennsylvania. Everything else rightfully belonged to Lizette.

Of course, when Felicity had gotten home shortly after Gage and Lizette had left, she'd protested loudly enough for the both of them. She'd even gone back into town, confronted Gage and Lizette at their hotel, and sought out the solicitor. Felicity had quickly learned that everything was true and that she and Patience were indeed homeless and penniless, that their uncle's will stated that the entirety of his land and all his belongings would go to his next of kin. And although the three young women were listed as beneficiaries, a daughter took precedence over nieces just as Gage had indicated.

Felicity had wired a telegram to Charity. But the return telegram from one of the Vanderwater family representatives had indicated that Charity and Hudson were still on their honeymoon and couldn't be reached.

Felicity had returned home livid, had stomped around and banged pots and pans as she'd set about getting supper simmering on the range still caked with tomato residue. After spending most of the afternoon protesting and trying to figure out what to do, Felicity had saddled old Stan again and ridden back to town.

Patience wasn't sure what her sister hoped to accomplish with the third trip of the day. But in the meantime, she'd decided to pack her art supplies. She would gladly leave everything else behind, but not the means of feeding her heart and soul. She would wither without the ability to be creative.

At the clomp of horse hooves in the wagon lane approaching the house, Patience grew motionless. The plod was more distinctive and heavier than Stan's.

Were Lizette and Gage returning already? Perhaps to oversee the packing and make sure she and Felicity didn't take anything?

Patience's gaze darted around. She had to hide her trunk of art supplies. Maybe if she covered the trunk with hay? Or with a blanket?

She palmed her forehead. She was a ninny to think a flimsy covering would keep anyone from searching the wagon. No, what she really needed to do was distract the visitor from coming into the barn altogether.

Hopping down from the wagon, she paused. What could she possibly do?

Her pulse began to hammer.

One of the young goats that had been born in June darted through the haymow and bumped against an open stall door. The rattle and clank echoed loudly enough to startle a mother tortoiseshell cat beside her litter of kittens. The mother hissed and growled at the goat, who backed up with a bleat and hurried away.

Kittens.

Patience started toward the stall with the kittens. She would gather up one and use it as a distraction. After all, who could resist a kitten? Especially when they were as adorable as this little family.

The four furry bundles were at least six weeks old, and one would be okay without its mama for a short while.

At the rap of a fist against the house door across the yard, Patience halted. The knocking was firm, determined, and purposeful, not at all like Gage or Lizette, who had entered the home as if it was already their own—because it was, in fact, already theirs.

Perhaps someone was coming to offer a solution for

her and Felicity.

Charity was the one with the boundless positivity, always seeing the best in others. Patience wasn't quite as optimistic and was more realistic. Even though she wanted to hope for the best in this current predicament, she guessed they would need a miracle.

Tucking the orange tabby into the crook of her arm, she padded lightly through the scattered hay and stepped into the open double doors. Sure enough, a horse was loosely tied to the hitching post out front. A man stood on the porch at the front door, waiting with a tense posture.

From the sweat-stained black Stetson on his head, the dark wool trousers with a light piece of leather sewn into the seat, and the spurs on his boots, she guessed he was a local ranch hand. They'd had plenty who'd come calling over the past year—some wanting to court them and still others proposing marriage right on the spot.

She and her sisters had been too new and too occupied with the boardinghouse to give the suitors serious consideration. At least, until the events of the past summer.

And now?

Maybe she needed to ride into town and accept one of the proposals that had been offered to her. There had been several over the summer, and one just last week as she'd been in town shopping for her art supplies. She hadn't known any of the men all that well. But unlike Charity, who'd wanted a fairy-tale romance, she would be satisfied with a simple marriage to a simple man.

Getting married would most definitely solve the problem of where to go and what to do now that she had nothing. She'd just have to make sure that the man whose proposal she accepted was willing to allow Felicity to live with them. She wouldn't get married to anyone who wasn't kind enough to shelter her sister too.

Whatever the case, she didn't need to worry about hiding her art supplies from Gage and Lizette at the moment. No distraction was necessary. Even so, she cuddled the kitten closer to her body and scratched behind its ears as it stared up at her with adoring eyes.

The man knocked again and then stepped back, rubbing at the back of his neck.

Patience cleared her throat.

The fellow pivoted. And she found herself gazing upon Mr. Spencer Wolcott, who owned the vast ranch to the south of their property. She'd recognize his handsome face anywhere. He had classic lines—well-defined cheekbones, a perfectly-sized nose, and a square jaw that was covered with a layer of scruff that matched his hair.

There was something about him that made her think of a medieval knight attired in plate armor and chain mail. Something noble and chivalrous yet strong.

Perhaps it was also because he always seemed so

serious. His forehead had perpetual creases, and his brows were always slanted downward. Not in a scowl, but as though the weight of the world rested upon his shoulders.

He watched her, seeming to take her in from her head to her toes.

After she'd cried off and on throughout the afternoon, her eyes were probably red-rimmed, her cheeks streaked, her nose puffy. Her apron was still stained from the charcoal and tomato sauce from earlier. And her hair? It was tied loosely in the braid that she always wore, but strands had come free and now blew about her face.

She guessed she looked a fright.

A strange sense of embarrassment wafted through her, and she wasn't sure why. She didn't care about impressing this man, did she?

From everything she'd heard, he was a man of upstanding character, and he'd never caused them any trouble as a neighbor. He'd visited their homestead once shortly after they'd moved to the area. And he'd asked them if they'd sell their land to him. When they'd told him no, he'd ridden off and hadn't pressured them since.

He hesitated a moment longer, then descended from the porch and began to cross the yard toward her. A dozen paces away, he stopped. "Miss Courtney?"

"Yes?"

"I'm Spencer Wolcott. I manage Trout Creek Ranch." He had a strong British accent. If she remembered correctly, he'd moved from England a couple of years ago. He seemed to be in his late twenties, perhaps early thirties.

And he was a widower. With a child. She did remember that, because he'd asked around for nursemaids for his child from time to time. From what she'd witnessed and heard, he was a loving father and cared deeply about his little girl.

Up close she could see that his eyes were green with hints of brown. And his hair was a dark brown beneath his hat.

He, too, seemed to be studying her more closely—her face, her eyes, her hair. What did he find lacking? Usually there was something wrong with her.

"How may I help you, Mr. Wolcott?"

His brows furrowed even deeper. And somehow it made him look even more attractive. "I heard about your predicament. And I am sorry you're losing your place."

"Thank you." The sincerity—and kindness—in his statement brought a fresh rush of tears to her eyes, and she had to blink to hold them back.

"Is your sister here?" He glanced around.

"No, she's in town."

He brought his attention back to her. "Has she—have you—made arrangements yet?"

"I'm afraid we're still figuring out what to do."

He lifted his hat and brushed through his hair, clearly

nervous. "I may have a solution."

"We'd welcome any ideas."

"I am looking for someone to come live at Trout Creek and take care of my daughter."

Was this a marriage proposal? She wasn't always sure with the men. "Under what capacity, Mr. Wolcott? As a nursemaid or wife?"

He hesitated, as though he wasn't sure of the answer himself. "What do you think would be the preference?"

Yes, she'd just told herself that she needed to go into town and accept one of the marriage proposals that she'd recently received. But was she really ready to make that next step? Especially to a man she hadn't spoken to before today?

Would she be better off becoming a nursemaid, at least until she could speak with Charity and discuss their financial situation? Charity certainly wouldn't want her to rush into a marriage like this.

At the same time, marriage would be a more permanent solution. She wouldn't have to worry about being a burden on Charity and Hudson, financially or otherwise. When they returned from the East, she'd have a place of her own, wouldn't be in their way, and wouldn't have to rely upon them for survival.

How could Charity fault a man like Mr. Wolcott? He was a prosperous rancher and would have the means to take care of them. Patience had seen him at church on occasion, and he seemed to be God-fearing. No one spoke poorly about him, at least that she'd heard.

"Would you allow us both to live at Trout Creek, Mr. Wolcott?"

"Certainly."

"It's just that Felicity is still so young, and I wouldn't feel comfortable allowing her to fend for herself." The kitten had fallen asleep in her arms, but she still scratched its back absently.

One of Mr. Wolcott's brows ticked upward. "Exactly how young is your sister, Miss Courtney?"

"Nineteen."

"Nineteen doesn't strike me as exceptionally young. Only nine years younger than me."

"And I assure you, my sister is mature. But I couldn't agree to the union unless the two of us can stay together."

"Then you think a marriage would be more agreeable to your sister?"

What would her sister say? Probably that they shouldn't be rash, that they'd hear back from Charity before long. And if they didn't get a response soon, they'd find other solutions besides marriage to the first man who offered them a home. Yet, Felicity would come around eventually, wouldn't she? "If she knows this is what I want, she'll agree to it."

"I have no wish to pressure her into this arrangement."

"She'll be fine." At least, Patience hoped so, especially because for some reason it seemed important to Mr. Wolcott that Felicity be in agreement to the union.

"Then you'll speak to your sister about it? Or shall I return later when she's home to discuss the matter with her myself?"

"No." Her voice came out slightly more emphatic than she intended. "I'll talk to her." The best plan was not to say anything until after the fact. Once she was safely married to Mr. Wolcott, then she would tell Felicity. At that point, her sister could protest all she wanted, but it would be too late.

"You're certain?" His expression was filled with sincerity. That had to be a good sign, didn't it?

Even so, could she really do this? Should she gather more information about him? About his ranching operations? About his child?

With his eyes upon her and filled with expectation, she wasn't sure how she could say no to him.

Earlier in the summer when they'd faced financial difficulties, she'd been ready and willing to accept marriage proposals from other men she didn't know all that well. Surely she could do so now.

The difference was that in the past, her sisters had been there to stop her from actually carrying through with her declarations. But this time, if she held back from telling Felicity about her plans, she'd have no one to jump in and keep her from making a mistake.

Would it be a mistake? Or did she dare go through with marrying him?

She finally nodded. Marriage was the best and most logical solution to their problem. "We'll meet at the church tomorrow morning at nine. Would that work for you, Mr. Wolcott?" She'd go early and meet with Father Zieber. If he had anything negative to say about Spencer Wolcott, she'd discover it then.

Mr. Wolcott rolled his shoulders as though attempting to dislodge the heavy burdens he carried. "I shall make nine o'clock work. And I would prefer it to be a simple ceremony."

"And quick."

He opened his mouth as if he wanted to say more, but then he paused. His brows slanted together again as he studied her face, this time lingering over her forehead, cheek, then chin.

What did he think of her? Was he attracted to her even a tiny bit? He must be a little, or he wouldn't have sought her out.

A flutter of warmth in her belly took her by surprise, and she could feel the bloom of that warmth begin to form in her cheeks. Maybe she needed to use the kitten as a distraction after all. She lifted the creature and pressed a kiss to its head.

As she did so, his attention shifted to the kitten. For

several long seconds, his gaze remained riveted to her lips brushing against the kitten's head.

When he finally tore his gaze away, he cast his sights down to the grass. "I shall see you and your sister tomorrow then, Miss Courtney." With that, he strode back to his horse with long and purposeful steps.

As he mounted, his trousers outlined legs honed with perfectly proportioned muscles. His coat stretched taut across his broad back and around his thickly corded arms, revealing more of the same strong body. Add to that the hard lines of his face covered in dark stubble and those beautiful sad eyes, and he was possibly the handsomest cowboy she'd seen since moving to Colorado.

Maybe she'd never imagined herself having a fairy-tale romance like Charity's, but she wouldn't protest having a husband who was fine to look at. Very fine indeed.

As soon as the thought came, embarrassment cascaded through her like pebbles at the beginning of an avalanche. Her thoughts were like those of a young girl, not a full-grown woman, and if she weren't careful to control them, she'd only cause a landslide and get hurt.

He nudged his heels into the horse's flank. At the same time, he tipped the brim of his hat at her politely before guiding his horse away.

She prayed he hadn't read her wayward thoughts. His appearance didn't matter. The important thing was that she was coming up with a solution to her problem. She was finding a way to provide for herself and Felicity. And she was doing it without Charity's help.

Now she just had to keep her plans to marry Mr. Wolcott from Felicity until after the wedding tomorrow. She'd never been good at deception, and she wasn't sure how she would manage to keep such a big secret. But she had to or risk Felicity interfering.

4

Spencer paused on the boardwalk outside the church door and stuck a finger in the collar of his shirt to keep it from strangling him.

Was he really doing this? Could he make himself go through with a wedding this morning?

He tugged the watch from his waistcoat pocket and examined the time. He'd arrived early and still had at least ten minutes.

He eyed his horse tied next to Tex's at the nearest hitching post. He could ride away and put an end to the madness. He'd simply go back to the ranch and put aside thoughts of marrying the redheaded Felicity Courtney.

After all, he hadn't even spoken to her about the marriage. He'd made all the arrangements through her sister. Tex had informed him the sister's name was Patience and that he thought she was the prettiest of the sisters.

Spencer could easily admit Tex was right. Especially after seeing her again last night. She'd been far too appealing standing in the barn doorway holding a kitten. She had lovely features—slender rosy cheeks, dainty nose and chin, and a graceful bearing.

Her blue eyes had been expressive—guileless and filled with curiosity. But there had also been something else entirely too alluring about them. Was it the long lashes? Or the heavy-lidded look, one that belonged in a bedroom? He guessed she hadn't meant to appear seductive and welcoming and ready to pull him down on top of her.

Tiny embers flared in his gut again like yesterday. But now, just as then, he mentally stomped out the glowing coals, unwilling to let them burn. He wasn't getting married for himself and the needs he'd kept locked away. He was doing it for Evangeline and only Evangeline.

And that's why he was marrying the redheaded sister and not the blond. Yes, Felicity was really pretty too, and he'd have to be careful not to get distracted with her either and stay true to his resolve. But there was something about Patience that had the potential to draw him more, maybe even make him half mad with need.

"Devil it." He swiped off his newest hat, a fine navy bowler that matched the navy suit he'd donned for the occasion. "What in the name of Zeus am I doing?"

Tex, attired in his simple but clean Sunday suit,

paused beside him.

Thankfully, Fairplay's Main Street wasn't overly busy. Very few would see him making a fool of himself outside the church—only a couple of wagons passing by, a few men loitering outside one of the hotels, and a mother and children going into a store.

"What's wrong, Mr. Wolcott, boss?" Tex had agreed to act as a witness to the wedding, and he'd assigned a couple other ranch hands, including Buck, to watch Evangeline—hopefully for only a short time. Before leaving, Buck had clamped him on the shoulder and told him he was doing the right thing.

Was he, though?

He was getting married to a woman he didn't know. One he'd never even talked to before in his life.

His lungs began to close up, choking off his air, making him feel as though he was drowning. The sensation came every once in a while, and he always hated how weak it made him feel.

Curses upon him. He was going home.

He spun on his heels and started back to his horse.

He made it two strides before Tex latched on to his arm and stopped him. "You've got to do this."

Spencer jerked to free his arm, and at the same time, dragged in a lungful of air past the tightness.

Tex didn't relent. "If you don't go in and marry that gal, you might as well shoot yourself in the foot—both feet—because you won't be able to do a blasted thing around the ranch."

"I'll tell her I'd rather just hire her as a nursemaid."

"Little Miss needs a mama." Tex's tone remained hard. "And you know it."

Spencer held himself rigid for another long moment and then let his shoulders slump under the weight of resignation. He'd thought about it all last evening and most of the restless night, and Tex was right. He had to go through with this. Evangeline needed a feminine influence who would train her and possibly even grow to love her.

He shifted back toward the church. Recently painted a fresh coat of white, it was a simple building with a short steeple—nothing like the magnificent old cathedral he'd gone to with his family.

Patience had assured him Felicity would agree, even be happy, to marry him. He may as well go inside and get situated before the two sisters arrived in town and found him outside acting like a mad old bat.

Squaring his shoulders, he forced himself to walk to the door, open it, and step inside.

The morning sunshine poured in through the windows and lit the place sufficiently without any lanterns, illuminating six worn pews on either side of a center aisle, old pictures of biblical scenes on the walls, and a simple altar at the front graced by a silver candelabra.

There, in front of the altar, stood Patience and Father Zieber. Patience took a rapid step away from the minister, her cheeks flushing. And Father Zieber closed his mouth without finishing whatever it was he'd been saying. Giant-sized, the man had thick hair that was graying, and he had kind and compassionate eyes.

Spencer halted just inside the doorway. "I beg your pardon. Shall I wait outside a moment while you finish your conversation?"

"No, no." Father Zieber waved him in. "I was just assuring Patience that you're a godly young man, that you'll make a fine husband."

Patience stood alone, without her sister, and was attired in a lovelier gown today than the one she'd worn yesterday. The satiny material was a bright blue, which only highlighted her big blue eyes. "Since I don't know you very well, I wanted to make sure Father Zieber approved of you."

"That's understandable." He spoke the words expected of him even though, once again, he had the urge to return to his horse and ride away.

Behind him, Tex gave him a sharp shove, giving him little choice but to plod down the aisle toward Patience and Father Zieber.

Where was Felicity?

He scanned the small church again but found no sight of her.

Perhaps she was merely running late. Or what if Patience hadn't been able to convince her to go through with the wedding yet? Maybe Felicity was waiting for her sister to return with all the information she'd gathered from Father Zieber before making up her mind.

The minister welcomed him with a warm smile. "For what it's worth, I believe you're doing the right thing in getting married, Mr. Wolcott. Your foreman explained the situation last night when he came calling to arrange the ceremony."

Buck had been the one to suggest lining up Father Zieber, and Tex had agreed. They'd wanted to make sure the minister was available, hadn't wanted to leave anything to chance. Or perhaps they'd hoped the solid plans would force Spencer to go through with it.

Father Zieber took a step toward the altar, opening up the spot next to Patience. "And you're certainly helping the Courtney sisters at a very difficult time."

"I'm hoping the union is mutually beneficial."

"Most marriages of convenience are."

Marriage of convenience. Was that what this was? Spencer hadn't really considered the matter, but he guessed both of them stood to gain something from the union.

A slight pinch of tension in his neck eased. Yes, they were both helping each other during difficult circumstances.

Father Zieber took a book from the pulpit and began to page through it. "I'm told you both want to keep the ceremony simple and short."

"Yes." He spoke the word at the same time as Patience.

"Then let's get started." The minister flipped through more pages.

Spencer glanced toward the window. No sight of Felicity.

"I normally prefer two witnesses," Father Zieber was saying, "but today, under the circumstances, we'll have just one."

Spencer lifted a brow at Tex. What was Father Zieber talking about?

Tex shrugged and peered out the window, clearly looking for Felicity too.

The minister smoothed a hand over the page. "Here we are. The order of service for Solemnization of Matrimony."

Patience didn't seem at all concerned that her sister was missing. She was, in fact, watching Father Zieber expectantly as if she intended to go through with the service without Felicity.

Spencer tugged out his watch again. It wasn't quite nine o'clock. She still had time to arrive. He started to expel a tense breath but sucked it in when the minister started reading from his book.

"Dearly beloved friends, we are gathered together here in the sight of God and in the face of this witness to join together this man and this woman in holy matrimony, which is an honorable state."

What in the devil was going on here?

Spencer cleared his throat loudly.

Father Zieber paused. "Is something the matter, Mr. Wolcott?"

"Shouldn't we wait for Felicity?" Didn't that seem obvious?

Patience shook her head. "She's not coming."

"She's not?" Again, Spencer glanced at Tex, hoping he wasn't the only one confused.

The old ranch hand's wiry brows were knit together, and his gaze was darting back and forth between Patience and him.

"We can't have a wedding without her." Spencer said the only thing left to say.

"We'll have to." Patience's cheeks were flushing a becoming shade of pink, and she was staring at her hands and twisting them together. "I admit, I didn't tell her yet."

"You didn't?" This was getting stranger by the moment.

"I know I said I would, but I don't want her to interfere. Once the wedding is over, then there won't be anything she can do to stop me."

"Stop you?" He fairly choked the words out.

"I'm afraid she won't approve"—finally Patience lifted her gaze to his, and as with yesterday, those sultry eyes stirred long-dormant heat inside him—"of my rash decision to marry you."

"Pardon?" She thought she was marrying him in place of Felicity? He started to shake his head, but Tex jabbed him hard in his ribs.

He pivoted and leveled a glare at his ranch hand, but Tex began dragging him away from the altar and toward a side door. Was he trying to help him escape?

"We'll be right back," Tex called toward Patience and the minister as he swung open the door.

Spencer was too confused by the state of events to do anything but follow dumbly along.

They exited into the narrow yard between the church and the business next door, and from all appearances they were alone.

Tex closed the door behind them as calmly as if a baby were sleeping on the other side. But in the next instant, he grabbed Spencer by both arms and thrust him back against the building. "What are you doing?" The darkness of Tex's glare warned Spencer not to play any games.

"I'm confused—"

Tex shook him and then nodded toward the closed door.

The message was clear. He needed to keep his voice low so that the minister and Patience weren't privy to their conversation.

He took a breath and started to speak again, but Tex beat him to it. "Now, listen to me, and listen good." The whisper was harsh.

Spencer started to throw off Tex's hold. "Release me. Now." He tolerated a great deal from the fatherly man, but he was crossing the line today.

Instead of letting go, Tex snatched a fistful of his shirt and pushed his face near enough that Spencer could smell the lingering scent of coffee on his breath. "You're going in there and marrying that girl. Do you hear me?"

Spencer narrowed his eyes into a glare that usually worked to bring even the wildest of cowboys into submission.

Tex shoved him again. "Do you hear me?"

Clearly his glare didn't work on Tex. "I said I'd marry Felicity—"

"Even if Felicity had shown up, I reckon we'd be out here having this conversation."

Spencer's ready retort died. Was Tex right? Was he looking for a way to sabotage the wedding this morning? Even so, he hadn't anticipated marrying Patience. She was too beautiful, reminded him too much of his late wife.

How had this mix-up taken place? Yes, he'd been nervous and had bumbled around with the conversation yesterday with Patience. But he'd mentioned Felicity many times, had assumed Patience knew that was who he was referring to during their entire discussion.

But apparently, she'd believed he was proposing marriage to her. What had he said to lead her to believe that?

He took off his hat and pinched the back of his neck. "I can't marry Patience."

Tex shrugged. "It could've been the other sister last night and this morning. But for whatever reason, the good Lord's brought this sister to you instead."

Spencer tilted his head back and stared up at the sky as if he could find the answer to his dilemma written there. But there was nothing.

"I can tell you already like her." Tex's whisper dropped. "And that's what's scaring you half to death."

For an old ranch hand, Tex had more insight than most. And he was probably right.

Did it really matter which sister he married? Whether he married Patience or Felicity, he wasn't planning to give his desires any latitude. It would be like a business arrangement for both of them and nothing more. With such an approach, hopefully he'd avoid all the theatrics he'd experienced with Honora.

"Very well." He was here, had taken the time to groom and get dressed up. He may as well accomplish the deed.

"You'll go back in there and marry the pretty lady?"

"Yes."

Tex's grip loosened, but he didn't let go all the way.

"I vow it." He met Tex's gaze and hoped the man could see the sincerity in his eyes.

Tex gave a curt nod, released him, then opened the door so that Spencer stumbled backward into the church.

Again, at the sight of him, Patience and Father Zieber—in the middle of another conversation—came to an abrupt halt.

"Is everything alright?" Father Zieber asked.

"It is now," Tex called in a too-cheerful voice.

Within moments, Spencer found himself back at the front of the church, standing beside Patience. He could feel her questioning gaze upon him, likely wondering what had happened. It was best if she didn't know he'd thought he was marrying Felicity. It would only make him look like an idiot. Besides, it was his fault. He'd been nervous yesterday and obviously hadn't made his intentions as clear as he'd needed to.

Thankfully, Father Zieber kept the service to the basics. They stated their intentions and made their vows. Then Father Zieber held out the prayer book in a silent signal that Spencer needed to put the wedding ring upon it.

Earlier, when he and Tex had left the ranch, Tex had asked him if he had a ring. Spencer hadn't wanted to admit that he'd tossed Honora's ring into the Atlantic during the voyage to America. And he'd had no reason to have another ring.

So the first place they'd stopped when they'd reached town had been Hyndman Bro's General Merchandise. Tex had sworn they sold rings. He'd been right. They'd found a delicate band with a simple sapphire at the center.

As he placed the ring onto the open page of Father Zieber's prayer book, he rubbed a finger over the sapphire. It was the same color as Patience's eyes. How had that happened? He certainly hadn't been drawn to the ring for that reason. Had he?

As he repeated the words after the minister, he tried not to look into her eyes, but he found himself gazing there regardless as she shyly peered up at him.

"With this ring, I thee wed," he said. "With my body, I thee worship. And with all my worldly goods, I thee endow. In the name of the Father and of the Son and of the Holy Ghost. Amen."

"Amen," she whispered.

He was trying not to overthink the vows, didn't want to start to panic again. But in this moment, with her beautiful eyes upon him, he prayed that God would help him to be a better husband than he'd been with Honora. At the very least he could hope that he didn't make an utter mess of things this time.

She held out her hand, and he slipped the ring on her finger as quickly as possible, trying to avoid touching her.

"It's lovely." She lifted her hand and examined the ring.

He opened his mouth to admit Tex had been the one to make him stop and purchase it. But at the nudge from Tex and a shake of his head, Spencer closed his mouth. For whatever reason, Tex didn't want to take credit for the ring. Even so, Spencer would figure out a way to thank the man for his help today, not only with the ring but for everything—the support, the encouragement, and yes, even the harshness to push him to do this for Evangeline.

The minister spoke the last words of the ceremony, and in an instant was signing the cross above them: "Those whom God hath joined together, let no man put asunder. I now pronounce that they be man and wife together."

With the benediction completed, Spencer stepped back only to have Tex thrust him toward Patience. "What about a kiss, Father Zieber—"

"No." Spencer shook his head, protest swelling inside. "We don't know each other yet."

Patience had ducked her head, the stain in her cheeks testifying to her innocence as well as her embarrassment.

Had she ever kissed a man?

His mind filled with the image of her yesterday

afternoon, standing in the barn door, her lips pressing against the kitten. The kiss, as innocent as it had been, had been much too enticing.

"No," he said again, needing to convince himself as much as Tex that he wasn't planning to kiss Patience.

"Aw, come on now." Tex knuckled his arm good-naturedly. "You may as well start now. Then you'll be ready for tonight."

"Zeus," Spencer muttered. He hadn't thought beyond the wedding ceremony to the marriage bed. He supposed at some point in the future, he'd share a bed with his wife. After all, he wasn't a monk. And no doubt she'd want to have a baby or two.

But for tonight? And anytime soon? He took another step away and this time avoided Tex. "Let's get back to the ranch. We have work to do."

Tex just grinned at him and waggled his eyebrows.

Patience kept her focus on the floor.

He needed to say something to her to ease the awkwardness. "You'll likely need to return to your home and retrieve your belongings."

She nodded.

"I'll send a couple of wagons and men to your home to help with the move."

Her shoulders seemed to ease their stiffness, and she offered him a smile, one filled with relief. "Thank you."

The tension inside him eased as well. He'd done the

right thing in showing consideration for her needs. All he had to do was more of the same.

With a nod at Patience, he started down the aisle toward the door. He needed to do better with this marriage. And then maybe this time he wouldn't drive his wife into the arms of another man.

As Felicity approached the wagon bench, Patience folded her hands in her lap and hid her new wedding ring.

Her stomach clenched. She'd done nothing wrong and had nothing to feel guilty about. In fact, she'd done the best thing for them both. Hadn't she?

Their worries were over. They would no longer be homeless. And Mr. Wolcott—Spencer—had even arranged for his men to come over and help move them.

Felicity climbed up the driver's side. She, too, had donned one of Charity's gowns for the morning—a lovely green color—and she looked exquisite. And worried. Very worried.

Last night, Felicity had returned from town still angry and discouraged by their predicament. This morning when she'd suggested they go into town to explore other living arrangements, Patience had breathed a sigh of relief that she wouldn't have to sneak away or make up an excuse to go into town for the wedding. In fact, Felicity had even been the one to suggest that they dress up in an effort to help their cause.

Felicity arranged her gown on the wagon seat before sitting down. Then she stared ahead, her lips set in a grim line. They'd parked their wagon on a side street, and in the August morning, only a few people were out and around town, which was just as well. Felicity hated the looks of pity. Not that Patience especially liked them, but she simply didn't notice the stares the way Felicity did.

"There's no need to worry, Felicity." Patience lifted a hand to rest it on Felicity's arm, but at the sparkle of the blue gem, she quickly snatched her hand back and buried it in her skirt. As soon as she did, she paused. Why was she trying to cover up the fact that she'd just gotten married? What was the point?

Since exiting the church a few minutes ago, Patience hadn't seen Spencer around town and guessed he'd already started home. She could admit she was slightly relieved that he and his companion weren't there to say anything about the wedding. Not yet.

She couldn't just spring the news on Felicity. She had to find a way to deliver the plan so that her sister didn't get angry.

"Everything's going to work out." Patience tried to infuse confidence into her tone. "You'll see."

Felicity gathered up the reins, released the brake lever,

and clucked the horses forward. "You're starting to sound like Charity—eternally optimistic."

"I have a good feeling about our situation." She had more than a good feeling. She had every certainty they would be well cared for by Spencer. Her meeting with Father Zieber before the ceremony had gone well. The reverend had known the man for the past two years since he'd moved from England and had spoken only positively about him.

He was honest, hard-working, and humble. His employees respected him because, although he required them to work hard, he treated them fairly and generously.

The only concern Father Zieber had was the hearsay from other smaller ranches. They didn't like that Trout Creek Ranch was growing into such a large venture and buying up more and more land. But Patience didn't see a problem with being ambitious.

In the end, Father Zieber had assured her that she couldn't go wrong with a union to a man of Spencer's high caliber and that she would eventually learn to love him. She hadn't argued with the pastor on that point. Especially since her attraction to Spencer had so easily sparked to life yesterday during their interaction.

She'd been too self-conscious during the wedding to feel those same sparks today. But she could admit he'd been just as handsome in his Sunday best as he'd been yesterday in his work clothing.

During the short, one-mile ride back to the homestead, Patience tried a dozen times to figure out how to tell Felicity she was married. Yet even as they drove into the barn, she still hadn't forced the words out.

Felicity was strangely quiet, her forehead marred by worry lines that a young woman her age shouldn't have to bear. Hopefully, her concerns would melt away soon enough, especially once they were living with Spencer.

As Felicity climbed down and started through the barn doors toward the house, her shoulders slumped with dejection.

Patience didn't move from the wagon seat. She needed to jump down and race after Felicity and say something. So why couldn't she? Was she afraid Felicity would march her back into town and demand an annulment?

Strangely, something inside her protested having to give up her new marriage to Spencer. She could admit she was fascinated by him. And the other truth was that he'd asked her to marry him. Her. Patience. Yes, she'd had proposals over the past year, but none from a man as handsome and successful as Spencer Wolcott.

Her mother had warned her that no decent man would want her for a wife, since she was so distractible, scattered, and clumsy.

Even now, from the grave, her mother's scolding echoed in her head, telling her Spencer wouldn't want her once he realized what she was really like. The voice chastised her for not being more honest with Spencer about her faults so that he knew the type of wife he'd gained.

"I'm going to improve." Her words echoed in the quiet barn.

Old Stan released a snort. Hopefully it was one of agreement.

"Just you wait." She began climbing down. "I can pay better attention and be less forgetful if I put my mind to it." She'd prove to Spencer that he hadn't made a wrong decision. She'd be a good mother to his daughter and a good wife to him.

A good wife.

She reached for the buckle of Stan's halter but then paused as embarrassed heat coursed through her. Spencer's friend at the wedding had mentioned something about the coming night. Although she was inexperienced, she guessed he was referring to the marriage bed and the act of procreating.

Even if the idea of sleeping with Spencer was mortifying and somewhat scary, she would do her wifely duty. And she wouldn't complain about it. Or at least, she wouldn't complain to him. Instead, she'd focus on trying to make him happy. She could do that, couldn't she?

After she took care of the horse, she set off for the

house. Most of what they owned was already packed in the trunks and crates stacked in the barn. But she had a few final personal and clothing items that needed to be tucked away.

In addition, Patience wanted to make sure everything was neat and clean for the new owners. Felicity hadn't wanted to make things easy on their cousin. But Patience had always taken to heart the Scripture verse that called on them not to repay evil with evil but rather with a blessing, and that's what she intended to do.

As she passed by the garden, a clump of weeds drew her into the plot that they'd cherished over the past summer. She plucked the weed only to discover that it had a vegetable of some sort growing on the end. She dusted off the lump, studied it, and then went in search of a tool to cut it in half and discover what it tasted like.

Back in the barn, she rummaged through the disorganized tools and finally found a spade. But in the process, the kittens decided they wanted to play, and before long she was involved in making an elaborate toy of braided rope and chicken feathers.

At the beat of horse hooves and wagon wheels drawing near, she jumped up and gasped. How much time had elapsed? She glanced around, taking in the position of the sun and the shadows. It couldn't be noon yet, could it?

The scattered mess of supplies was spread out in front

of her, and the kittens watched her expectantly. She tenderly rubbed the nearest one. "I'm sorry. I don't have time to finish."

She quickly swiped up as many as she could hold of the miscellaneous items and started toward the door. As the rumbling wagon rolled to a stop, she dumped everything on the closest shelf.

"May I help you?" came Felicity's call.

"We're here to collect Mrs. Wolcott," a man responded, "and help her move her belongings."

Patience drew in a sharp breath. Spencer's men were here. And now Felicity knew that she'd gotten married.

A long pause ensued, one in which Patience could hear each thudding beat of her heart. What was going through Felicity's head?

"I'm sorry." Felicity's tone was polite. "You've come to the wrong place. There's no Mrs. Wolcott here."

"Is this the Courtney homestead?" the man asked, his voice ringing with confusion.

"Yes."

"Then we're in the right place."

"We have no Mrs. Wolcott staying with us."

No, no, no. Apparently Felicity didn't understand what was going on.

Another silence fell, and Patience started toward the door. She had to confess now, or Felicity would end up sending the men away.

The man spoke again. "If Mrs. Wolcott isn't here, can you tell us where we can find her?"

"I have no idea—"

"Here." Patience pushed through the barn door, even though her footsteps seemed to want to drag her the opposite way. "I'm here."

Felicity stood on the front porch, hands on both hips. Hatless but still in her fancy gown, she looked older than her nineteen years. Frazzled, frustrated, and feisty. And now her narrowed gaze swung to Patience. "You're not Mrs. Wolcott."

Patience swallowed the lump that lodged in her throat. "Actually, I am. I married Mr. Wolcott this morning at the church in Fairplay."

Felicity shook her head. Then with widening eyes, she took in the two men and the empty wagons before returning her gaze to Patience.

Patience did the only thing she knew to do. She held up her hand and showed the ring. Of course, across the yard they were too far apart for Felicity to see the details of the beautiful ring. But nevertheless, the sunlight glinted off the jewel, turning it into a lighthouse beacon.

"You got married this morning?" Felicity's voice rang with shock.

"I made the arrangements with Mr. Wolcott late yesterday afternoon when he called on me and suggested that I marry him."

"You accepted a proposal from a man you don't know?"

"Don't worry. I spoke at length with Father Zieber about him, and now I know him to a small degree."

"To a small degree?"

The gazes of the two men swung back and forth between her and Felicity. What must they be thinking of the whole exchange?

Patience swallowed her hesitation and kept going. Now that the news was out, she had to convince Felicity this was the best option. "Most importantly, Mr. Wolcott has agreed to allow you to come live with me. I told him I couldn't accept his proposal any other way." She hadn't said so in those exact words, but he'd seemed to be just as concerned about Felicity as she was.

Felicity stared at her for a long moment. Then she pressed her hand to her forehead. "Oh dear heavens, what am I going to do?"

"You're going to come live with me at Trout Creek Ranch. That's what you're going to do."

"That's not what I meant." She heaved an exasperated sigh. "I'm trying to figure out what to do with you."

"With me?"

Felicity stared at the wagon path that led to town, her brow furrowing. "You can go get an annulment. That's what."

Just the thing she'd predicted Felicity would say. As

hard as it would be, she had to stand up to her sister, couldn't let her dictate the situation. "I don't intend to get an annulment."

"You can stay at the Hotel Windsor for a few days." Felicity continued as though she hadn't heard Patience. "Mr. Fehling said he'll accept payment for your room after we hear back from Charity or Hudson."

"I can handle things fine, just like Charity. Well, maybe not just like Charity. But she's not the only one who can solve problems." For too long, she'd lived in Charity's shadow, maybe even Felicity's. And in the shadow, she was always falling short. Maybe this marriage would help her gain her own footing, her own life.

"Yes, you'll take a room in the hotel," Felicity insisted. "And I have a job lined up to be a companion to Mrs. Bancroft."

Was that what Felicity had been doing during her trips to town? Looking for employment?

"Mrs. Bancroft has agreed to hire me and let me live with her, but she won't allow you to live at her house too." Mrs. Bancroft was one of the wealthiest ladies in town, a widow with a penchant for art and music and parties. She wasn't necessarily a warm and welcoming person.

"Do you want to work for Mrs. Bancroft?"

"Yes, I do. She's promised that I can travel with her next time she goes to Europe." Felicity's eyes sparkled at the prospect.

Patience had never understood her sister's longing to travel and have adventures. But she prayed that being Mrs. Bancroft's companion would give her new opportunities.

"I just want to make sure you're taken care of too." This time Felicity's words softened, as did her expression. She started down the porch and began crossing the yard toward Patience. Her steps were as firm and determined as always. She didn't stop until she reached the barn door and was but a foot away.

"You don't have to rush into a marriage to save us, Patience." The morning sunshine turned Felicity's red hair into a stunning auburn and lightened the brown of her eyes to warm molasses. "We can make it work another way."

"This is what I want." She'd much rather be married to Spencer and live at Trout Creek Ranch than stay indefinitely in a hotel.

Felicity studied her face for a moment, then sighed. "You know Charity will be livid if I let you go through with this."

"Charity doesn't always know what's best for me."

"She knew that if something like this happened, you'd be willing to settle for just about anyone."

"I'm not picky." She couldn't afford to be. Otherwise she might never end up with a husband.

"Charity—and me too—we just want you to find a

man you love and who loves you in return."

Patience shrugged. "Not all of us can expect that kind of marriage."

Felicity lifted her hand and cupped Patience's cheek. "You're a beautiful, talented, and kind woman. I wish you could see that you deserve more."

Patience pressed her hand over Felicity's. "I'll be fine. I don't need much to make me happy."

"So I can't stop you from doing this?"

"I need to be on my own now. Without you and Charity always looking out for me."

With a sigh, Felicity stepped back. "Then I guess it's time we each go our separate ways."

Patience nodded. It was indeed. And it was time for her to start her new life as Spencer Wolcott's wife.

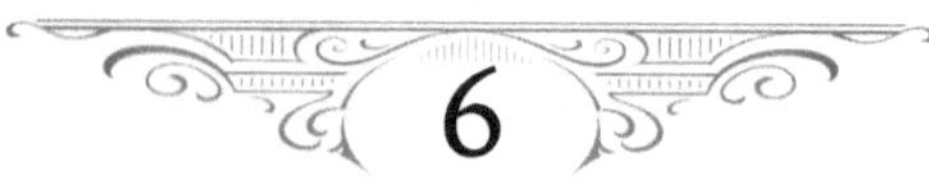

6

Patience clung to the wagon bench more tightly as the wagon lumbered closer to the ranch house. Trepidation raced along her nerves. Had she made the right decision?

The grassy yard surrounding the house was overgrown and dry with a dirt walkway leading to the front porch. No flowers, no decorations. Not a drop of color in sight.

But the porch did have a bench swing hanging from chains from the ceiling. And a little girl sat on it pushing it back and forth.

At the sight of the wagon, she thrust off in a daring, almost dangerous, jump. In the next instant she was racing down the steps and onto the dirt path, shouting at a nearby paddock.

Two large barns sat a short distance from the house and were surrounded by a series of corrals. A dozen or more cattle were congregated together in one, and several ranch hands were pinning a bellowing steer down on the ground while another man held one knee against the creature's ribs. She couldn't determine what they were doing, but she could see from the build and confident mannerism that the man on top was Spencer.

He'd obviously changed out of his Sunday attire and was back in his dark trousers, a flannel shirt, and Stetson. He had a bandana pulled up over his mouth and nose, which was no surprise since the dust was swirling in the air throughout the paddock, attesting to the dryness of the land at the end of the summer.

The little girl bounded toward Spencer, waving her arms and shouting. Her hair was uncombed and tangled, her feet bare, and the gown she was wearing was much too small.

Although Spencer hadn't mentioned the little girl's name or age or anything about her, Father Zieber had informed Patience that the child was called Evangeline, was four years of age, and was quite precocious and in need of womanly influence.

Father Zieber seemed to be right.

Patience hadn't been around children since arriving in Fairplay, but she'd had plenty of experience in watching and playing with children when she lived in Pennsylvania. Not only had she kept her cousins occupied during their family gatherings, but she'd also often taken care of the young children during the weekly Quaker meetings.

Now, at the sight of the girl, tenderness filled her

heart. Poor sweet child. She was as untended and neglected as the house and yard and was in need of a little nurturing and brightening.

Patience knew she wasn't good at many things, but she didn't doubt that she could bring new life to the girl and the home. Perhaps not in the conventional way that others would approve of. Instead, she often viewed people as she did her art: requiring splashes of color, texture, and vibrancy, like a mural in need of a fresh design. The possibilities were endless.

Had Providence arranged this partnership with Spencer for this very reason, so that she could create beauty in the desolateness?

A small thrill wound through her body. As the wagon rattled to a stop near the house, she didn't wait for the driver to come around and help her. She climbed down eagerly and started toward Evangeline, who was waiting by the corral fence for her father but had now turned to watch her approach.

"Papa, she's coming!" Evangeline called.

Spencer was still kneeling against the steer, his focus entirely on his work. He didn't even seem to notice that Evangeline was waiting for him.

Patience admired anyone who could focus so intently. It was so opposite of her own distractibility. Even as she crossed to Evangeline, she couldn't keep from noticing several apple trees among the other trees that surrounded the house. They were laden with the ripening fruit, and her mind pictured them sliced and dried and hanging in a garland above the hearth.

Patience pushed the vision from her mind and instead smiled at the little girl. Evangeline had blue eyes that were the hue of sea glass, blond hair that was sun-bleached to the color of pale butter, and delicate features like those of a porcelain doll. And even though she had dust smudged on her cheek and nose, she was beautiful.

Evangeline's coloring was so opposite of Spencer's darker hair and eyes that Patience guessed the child resembled her mother. What did the child remember—if anything—of her mother? And was she ready for a new woman in her life? Or would she be like the children in storybooks who had a difficult time adjusting to a stepparent?

She stopped in front of the girl and crouched so that she was on the same level. "Hello, Evangeline. I'm Patience, your new mother."

Evangeline's eyes were wide. "You're too young to be my mama."

Patience held back a laugh. "I'm twenty-one. I think that's old enough, don't you?"

"I guess so."

"Papa said you'd have red hair."

Red hair? That was strange. "No, mine is the same color as yours, or fairly close."

Evangeline studied her with eyes that slanted in a similar fashion to Spencer's. "I suppose that's better. Then people will think you're my real mama since we look alike."

"That would be really nice. I'd like that."

"You would?" The girl's eyes filled with hope, so much that Patience could feel the sting of tears forming in her eyes.

"I want you to always love your other mother. But I'd like it if you consider me your mother now."

At the growing silence of the men in the corral, Patience cast them a glance to find that the ranch hands were staring at her. Spencer had finally risen from the steer and was wiping his face with his sleeve while watching her interact with Evangeline.

What was he thinking?

His expression didn't give anything away. And as he climbed over the fence and hopped down to stand beside Evangeline, he seemed guarded. Was he having second thoughts about their marriage? Did he regret it already?

"I see you've met Evangeline." He patted the girl's head.

Patience straightened and tried to ignore the feeling that she was on display to the entire ranch and waiting for their approval.

"Can I call you Mama?" Evangeline blurted.

Spencer winced imperceptibly. Was it too painful for

him to think about his daughter calling another woman the term of endearment?

Patience hesitated. "I'm willing for you to call me Mama, but we need to make sure that's okay with your papa first." As she spoke, she tried to figure out Spencer's reaction.

He gave none, at least that she could tell.

"Can I, Papa? Can I call her Mama?" Evangeline's tone was threaded with an eagerness that warmed Patience's heart.

As if sensing the same eagerness, Spencer rustled her hair again. "If you wish."

Evangeline gave a cheer, then clasped Patience's hand. "We're going to show you the house . . . Mama."

Patience squeezed the girl's hand and then held on to it. "I'd like that. You can show me your room and all of your things."

They started forward, but then Evangeline stopped and reached a hand back toward Spencer. "You said we could show her together."

Spencer hesitated a moment, glanced at the cowhands still all unabashedly staring at them, then took Evangeline's outstretched hand. "I don't have long, Evangeline."

"We need to make her feel welcome, Papa." The child's voice held censure. "So that she wants to stay with us."

"No need to worry." Patience let Evangeline swing her arm as they began to walk toward the house. "I'm not planning to go anywhere."

"All my nursemaids leave." Evangeline skipped between her and Spencer, kicking up dust.

"That's why I married your papa. Because then I don't have to leave. I can stay with you forever."

Evangeline's smile broke through, but it seemed tentative, as though she hadn't smiled in a while. Patience guessed Spencer hadn't smiled in a while either. Maybe it was time to change that for both of them.

As they drew near the house, a strange sense of belonging, even satisfaction, fell over Patience. With Spencer on the opposite side of Evangeline, swinging arms too, Patience could almost believe that they were a family, that she was where she needed to be, and that this could grow into something beautiful.

When they reached the house, Evangeline broke loose and raced up the porch stairs. "Look! I can hop two at a time."

Before Patience could respond, Spencer leaned in. He nodded toward the wagon the men were unloading with her few trunks and bags. "I see you only needed one of the wagons."

"I didn't have much." Patience could feel the heat radiating from him, the August sun hot at midday. She caught a waft of his cologne—a musky, spicy scent. It had been much stronger at the church this morning, so much so she'd been tempted to move closer to him a time or two just to breathe him in.

"I don't see your sister," he said in a whisper. "Am I to presume she'll be coming later?"

"She's made other arrangements, actually."

One of Spencer's brows quirked.

It was a look that tugged at her insides and made her want to keep on gazing at him and all his handsomeness. But that was a silly notion, and she had to be careful about getting carried away.

"Then she didn't take the news of your matrimony well?" He kept his voice low with a glance toward Evangeline, who was heading for the porch swing and clamoring for the two of them to join her on it.

"In the end, she accepted my decision."

"Good."

Was he relieved not to have to worry about a disgruntled sister trying to interfere with their marriage? Or was he glad Felicity wasn't coming to live at the ranch?

Patience had never been proficient at reading people's emotions. She'd learned over the years to do so with Charity and Felicity. Maybe she'd eventually learn to understand Spencer.

He waved his hand toward the steps. "Shall we?"

She couldn't keep from pausing for a moment and

taking in the wide steps, the boards gray and weathered. They would look pretty in a fresh coat of primary blue paint. And the shutters beside the windows needed to be blue too. She could fashion several stained glass-like lanterns with different shades of blue glass to hang from the rafters. She had some left from a previous project.

Spencer's brow rose higher.

She gave herself a mental shake. She couldn't get distracted today. Especially not now. Instead, she had to show him she was capable of being a mother and could handle every aspect of it.

She hurried up, her heart swelling with purpose and the thrill of the challenge ahead. She sat on the swing next to Evangeline. A moment later, Spencer took the spot on the other side of the child. Evangeline chatted easily, telling Patience all about the swing and how she'd fallen off it and cut her chin once.

As the ranch hands clomped up the steps with one of her trunks, Patience rose and rushed to the door, swinging it wide for them.

"Where to?" the first man asked.

"I'm not sure." Where did Spencer want her to keep her clothing and belongings? In his bedroom? The very thought sent a rush of embarrassment through her.

Spencer hesitated. "The main bedroom is on the first floor. Second door on the left."

"That's Papa's." Evangeline hopped off the swing the

same way she had earlier and raced across the porch. Her little hand slipped into Patience's and tugged her through the door after the ranch hands. "You're lucky you get to share a room with him."

The insinuation from the wedding came back to Patience as it had earlier. From now on, she would spend her nights beside Spencer in his bed.

Goodness gracious. She dipped her head, unable to look back at Spencer and gauge his reaction to the arrangements.

"Come on." Evangeline guided her into the narrow front hallway, which was barren, without a single decoration or wall hanging—only a plain rug in front of the door.

A parlor and a dining room occupied the front rooms of the house across the hallway from each other. From what she could tell with only a quick glance, they contained fine furniture—mahogany upholstered in fine damask. Other than a gilded mirror above a fireplace, nothing else brought life to the rooms. They had no character, no voice, no style. Nothing.

It was almost as if the person who lived in the home hadn't expected to truly set down roots, had only anticipated it being a temporary lodging. Or perhaps the home was neglected because it lacked a woman's touch.

As Evangeline led her after the ranch hands toward an open doorway near the end of the hallway, her steps faltered. Was she really ready for this?

Even if not, she couldn't change her mind. She was already married. Like it or not, sharing a bedroom with a man was her fate, and she would have to make the best of it.

Evangeline didn't hesitate to enter the bedroom, dragging Patience behind her in time to see the ranch hands lower the trunk against the wall farthest from the bed. The bed. Thankfully it was a fairly big size. It was neatly made with a dark-blue cover, much more neatly than Patience ever made her own bed.

As with the other rooms, the bedroom was simple and unadorned, with a tall chest of drawers with a few men's toiletries arranged on the top. The bedside table contained a simple lamp and a stack of books. And a large trunk stood against the baseboard.

Evangeline raced across the room and launched herself onto the bed, laughing and rolling around. "Come join me, Mama. It's a really nice bed."

Patience hesitated.

"No, Evangeline." Spencer's voice in the doorway behind her turned stern.

Evangeline sat up, her hair messier than before—if that were even possible. Even so, the picture she made in the middle of the bed was portrait worthy. Patience would have liked to freeze the moment and capture it in paint. But alas, she'd never been particularly good at drawing or painting likenesses of people.

"Let's show your new mother the upstairs." Spencer was already backing out of the room as though he couldn't leave fast enough. Was he embarrassed by the prospect of sharing a bed with her too?

The tour of the rest of the house didn't last long. They peeked into the kitchen, which connected to the dining room. Spencer indicated that they didn't have a private cook and instead took most meals with the ranch hands in their dining hall, where a German cook and his assistant were in charge of preparing three meals a day for all the men who lived and worked on the ranch.

The gabled upstairs consisted of two bedrooms—one that the nursemaid had used, which was now empty, and one that belonged to Evangeline. Patience could see that someone, perhaps one of the nursemaids, had attempted to make the room cozy for a little girl, filling it mostly with lace and everything white—a white bedspread, white curtains, a white rug, white furniture.

Even though it was pretty, a child like Evangeline needed color—bright ones in every hue. As Patience stood in the highest point of the slanted ceiling, her mind went to work creating a room that would be perfect for the girl.

As she traced her hand over the plain wall, she barely heard Spencer indicate that he needed to return to work. And as she began to describe to Evangeline the enchanted forestland that she wanted to design, everything else fled from her mind.

Thankfully, Evangeline was enraptured with all the ideas. As they set out to find supplies for various projects, Evangeline didn't seem to mind that Patience stopped to admire the gardens and then got distracted by the pony. She showed Evangeline how to comb the pony's mane and braid ribbons in it, which led to washing and combing Evangeline's hair and putting ribbons in it. The ribbons reminded Patience of a fun game she'd once made with ribbons and buttons. And by the time they'd created the game, Patience remembered that she wanted to work on Evangeline's bedroom.

As Patience opened her craft trunk in the main bedroom and began to pull out paints and brushes, Evangeline's eagerness warmed her heart. No condemnation for getting distracted. No scolding for the messes she'd left behind. And no worrying about the time.

Patience had the feeling she would love being a mother. If only she felt the same anticipation about being a wife.

7

As Spencer stepped through the front door, the quiet and calm of the house sent alarm through him. Maybe he'd been hasty in leaving Patience alone with Evangeline so quickly after her arrival. Perhaps he should have spent a little more time with them both to ensure that Patience could manage Evangeline.

In fact, the guilt had been building all afternoon, especially the guilt that he hadn't warned Patience of what a handful Evangeline could be. He should have told her yesterday when he'd made the arrangements. But then, of course, he hadn't realized he was proposing marriage to her, had believed he was marrying her sister.

He glanced into the dining room and then into the parlor without sight of anyone. At the creak of footsteps overhead and the quiet murmur of voices, he expelled a taut breath. That had to be them in Evangeline's room.

How had Patience managed?

Most nursemaids were frazzled by the end of their first day of attempting to wrangle Evangeline and get her to behave as a proper young girl. Evangeline rarely cooperated, especially with baths and grooming.

He started toward the narrow stairway at the back of the house that led to the upstairs. As he neared his bedroom, he paused. He'd been put on the spot earlier by the ranch hands regarding where to put Patience's trunks. He hadn't wanted to tell them to carry everything upstairs to the spare room. If everyone learned that he'd relegated his wife to a different bedroom, the rumors would start flying.

He didn't mind gossip about himself, never paid it any heed. But he didn't want to bring any disgrace or harm to Patience's reputation on the ranch. Now that she was his wife, he wanted the men to respect her.

So he'd done the only thing he could think of. He'd pretended he was having Patience share a room with him. But there was no way he was ready for that. Not now. And not for a long time.

He'd have to let her know she should take the bedroom next to Evangeline's for the time being. And he'd have to come up with an excuse for the change in sleeping arrangements that Evangeline would accept. How was it that a girl her age already expected him to share a bed with his wife? Had she overheard the men in their coarse talking?

A sliver of frustration needled him. He'd made it clear to all the ranch hands that they were to watch their language and conversations around his daughter.

Whatever the case, in spite of Evangeline's expectations, he had to move Patience's belongings to the other bedroom. He'd do so tonight. After supper.

As he passed by his room, he glanced inside to get a count of how many trunks and the sizes. Would he be able to carry them by himself?

At the sight of the mess that met him, he frowned. The trunks were open. Items spilled over the edges and littered the floor. The bed was also covered in ribbons and buttons and other items he couldn't begin to name.

What had happened? Had Evangeline rummaged through Patience's belongings and made the mess? He'd have to chastise her and make her go back down and put everything away. Hopefully Patience wouldn't be too upset with the child.

With a sigh of discouragement, he made his way up the stairs. As he reached the top, he glimpsed Patience straight ahead, standing in the middle of Evangeline's room, her head cocked as she stared at something. She was wearing an apron tied over the same pretty gown that she'd worn to the wedding. But her sleeves were pushed up, and her hands and arms were splattered with . . . paint?

He started down the hallway, his footsteps loud

enough to warn her of his coming. But she didn't seem to hear him, was too focused on whatever she was looking at. Even as he stepped into the doorway, she didn't notice him.

Evangeline, in front of the same wall that Patience was staring at, swiveled with a paintbrush in hand. "Hello, Papa. We're painting."

In that moment, Patience startled, and her big blue eyes shifted to him. His breath hitched, as it seemed to be doing every time he gazed directly upon her. How had this exquisitely lovely woman still been available yesterday when he'd met her? How had some other man not married her already?

Even with her hair coming loose from the fashionable style and hanging in disarray, and even with the splatter of blue paint on the tip of her nose, she was perfectly beautiful.

Perfectly beautiful. Just like Honora.

He frowned and shifted his attention to Evangeline, this time taking note of the paint splatters on her face and hands. And the wall . . .

"What in the devil—" He quickly stopped himself. The vulgarity slipped out too easily, one he shouldn't be using around women. "What is the meaning of this?" He waved a hand at the bright colors slathered into what appeared to be a drawing of some kind. Trees? Flowers? Butterflies? A pony?

And the mess? Open paint tubes, discarded brushes, charcoal pencil stubs, more ribbon, wads of newspaper, rags, and other items littered the place. At least a layer of canvas had been laid across the floor.

Evangeline turned an adoring gaze upon Patience. "Mama is turning my bedroom into an enchanted forest."

Patience gave him a weak smile. "I didn't think to ask you. I'm sorry."

He took a deep breath to calm his quickly fraying nerves. He prided himself on being a man of orderliness and neatness, running his ranch with carefully calculated decisions, organization, and routine.

This—he glanced around again at the disaster that had taken over Evangeline's room—was far outside the scope of his comfort.

"What do you think, Papa?" Evangeline stood back to reveal the part of the wall she'd been painting. "Isn't it pretty?"

With a furrowing brow, he started to shake his head. But his attention snagged upon Evangeline's neatly styled hair, ribbons threaded throughout. And her face. Clean of the dirt and grime that had been a permanent fixture there. She was also wearing shoes. He couldn't remember the last time he'd been able to coerce her into putting on shoes, other than for church on Sundays.

How had Patience managed the transformation in one afternoon when none of the nursemaids had made progress after days—even weeks—of nagging?

Patience had begun to hurriedly clean up, swiping up brushes and rags.

Did it really matter that she was painting the wall in Evangeline's room? If it made Evangeline happy, wasn't that important? And if it had somehow allowed Patience to magically make Evangeline willing to groom herself, then who was he to question her methods?

The anticipation on Evangeline's face slipped away, and her dainty shoulders began to slump. She placed her brush down onto a strip of newspaper, clearly feeling his disappointment.

He shook off the strange sense of watching from a distance. Then he mustered up what he hoped was appropriate enthusiasm. "It looks like you and your new mama have been having fun together."

Evangeline's shoulders bounced back up. "Loads of fun, Papa."

"It's an . . . interesting project, to be sure." *Interesting* was a mild description for the chaos. "As long as you're careful, I give you permission to continue it." The endeavor was certainly preferable and tamer than loitering with the ranch hands and imitating their coarse deeds.

Patience slid him a sideways look, one filled with uncertainty.

"Thank you, Papa." Evangeline looked more mature, or perhaps she was acting more mature. Whatever it was, he could already sense Patience's influence upon her. "You're going to love it when we're all finished."

"Perhaps I shall." He doubted it. But what harm could come of giving Patience leeway with the child?

Patience continued to clean up silently.

"I came to gather you for supper. Can you leave your work of art for a short while for the evening meal?"

Evangeline glanced at Patience, clearly waiting to take cues from her new mama.

Patience pressed a hand to her forehead. "Goodness gracious. I completely forgot about eating."

She rapidly wrapped up the paintbrushes and then wiped a drop of paint from Evangeline's face. A moment later, as they started toward the stairs past the spare room, Spencer halted Patience with a slight touch to her elbow.

"I'm sorry," she whispered with a glance toward Evangeline, who was already hopping down the steps and making frog noises. "Sometimes I get carried away—"

"No harm done." He nodded at the empty nursemaid room. "I'll move your trunks and bags to this room later."

She glanced inside. "I did bring an awful lot. And perhaps it would be more convenient to have my supplies closer to Evangeline's room."

"Yes, precisely. Since my room is so crowded . . . and we still need time to get to know each other . . ."

She nodded, her cheeks flushing slightly. "I understand."

Was she relieved he was giving her a room of her own for now?

The blue paint spot on Patience's nose beckoned him. And before he could stop himself, he reached up and brushed his thumb across it.

At the touch, she froze.

The softness of her skin, the warmth of her breath against his wrist, the wideness of her eyes watching him and filled with such innocence—it all was like a red-hot branding iron searing through rawhide, sizzling, smoking. Just this miniscule contact with her was swirling up desires he'd thought were extinct and buried under layers of sediment.

He had the sudden longing to rub his thumb across her cheek, then her ear, and perhaps down her neck. He would wipe away every last fleck of paint and then some.

She opened her mouth as though to say something, but her lips stalled.

His attention shifted from her nose to her parted lips. They were perfectly rounded and curved and would probably be soft and pliable.

With an almost frustrated growl, he dropped his hand. What in the devil was he doing touching her so familiarly? He could have just mentioned that she had a splatter on her nose and let her wipe off her own face. Instead, he was reviving physical cravings that needed to remain embedded in the layers of sandstone where they belonged.

He backed up a step and waved her ahead of him. She watched him another moment, her eyelids lowering in that sensual way that made her look as if she needed to be swept off her feet and deposited into his bed.

Deposit her in his bed? Curses upon him. What was wrong with him that his mind kept wandering so lustfully?

It had to be because she was so lovely, so captivating, that his brain was having trouble working correctly every time he was around her.

He shifted his attention to the empty bedroom, trying to think, trying to make his mind move on to anything else but her. His sights landed on the bed. Another bed. Another opportunity . . .

No. He shook his head almost angrily.

As if sensing the ancient beast of longing rising to life inside him and needing to escape, Patience hurried toward the stairway, her footsteps slapping lightly against the wood floor.

Taking deep breaths, he waited in the hallway. He'd already decided it was best for him, for her, for them both, if he kept their marriage relationship one that was in name only. And that meant he also had to keep his thoughts in strict line, had to get out the cat-o'-nine-tails and flog his desires into submission.

He only descended when he could hear her talking with Evangeline. As they walked the short distance to the cook's house and the dining hall, Evangeline provided enough chatter and distraction—or mostly so—to keep his thoughts in order.

The ranch hands were already busy eating when he entered with Patience and Evangeline. The tables and benches were pushed together to make two long rows in a simple but spacious room. Bowls and platters filled the centers of both tables, and the scent of fried fish told him tonight's meal was trout caught from the stream after which the ranch was named.

The cook was decent enough—better than the previous fellow. Rather than the same old beans and bacon or roast and potatoes, the cook added variety to the menu, which was something the workers appreciated.

As Spencer began to cross to the table where he always sat, the room grew so quiet that the cook's rapid conversation in German filtered into the dining hall from the kitchen.

With forks suspended, all eyes turned toward him. Rather, toward Patience.

She didn't seem to notice the attention she was drawing, was focused on something Evangeline was saying.

But Spencer noticed. He could see the appreciation lighting up eyes, even the lust formulating in some. And the very thought that anyone else was looking at Patience drove a cattle prod straight inside him.

Even if she was a very fine woman to admire, the men needed to keep their eyes off her. She belonged to him now. And he wouldn't stand for any other man looking at her or talking to her. The interactions all started so harmlessly, but he'd learned just how rapidly such innocence could lead to more.

He slipped his hand to the small of her back. Although his fingertips barely skimmed the low spot above her waist, the brush against her smacked into him as hard as a mallet against a fence post.

The slight contact brought her up right away, drawing her wide, beautiful eyes directly to his face.

Was she sensitive to his touch?

She was peering at him with expectation, as though she sensed something was amiss inside him and wanted to fix it.

Nothing was amiss except his irrational need to show his men that his new wife was off-limits to them. But he couldn't very well tell her that. Instead, he cocked his head toward the table where he and Evangeline usually sat next to Tex and Buck. The spots were empty and another place open—the place where Tex normally sat. The older man had moved down a position and was the only one eating, as though the boss made an everyday occurrence of bringing a woman to dinner with him.

Evangeline was already bounding over to Tex, which led directly into her retelling of her afternoon with

Patience and the enchanted forest they were making in her bedroom.

Spencer kept his hand on Patience's back, leveled what he hoped was a serious warning to all the men present, then guided her toward their spots.

She didn't say anything as she took the seat next to Evangeline. She was finally looking around the dining hall and taking in the men, who had thankfully dropped their gazes to their plates, heeding his glare.

All except Buck. The ranch foreman still had his eyes on Patience as if she were the dessert being served to him on a silver platter.

As Spencer passed by Buck, he bumped the man hard, hoping he'd get the message not to look at Patience again.

With frustration pooling inside, Spencer lowered himself into the chair beside Patience. This would be the last meal he ate in the dining hall with the men. From now on, he'd instruct the cook's assistant to deliver a portion of the meal to the house, where he'd dine with his wife and daughter in private.

Even if his marriage was mainly for Evangeline to have a mother, he wasn't taking any chances this time. He was safeguarding what was his.

He didn't realize he'd brushed his hand over her arm almost possessively until she focused on him again, her eyes seeming to ask him what was wrong.

He didn't know what to tell her, so instead, he forced

himself to move away, reach for his fork, and pretend that everything was alright. But somehow he sensed that he'd upset the balance in his life with the rash decision to get married, and he wouldn't be the same ever again.

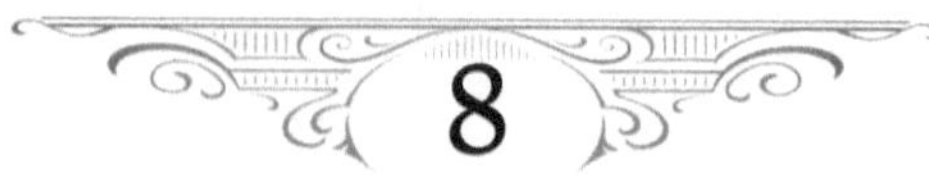

8

Patience was avoiding going to bed. She could admit it. The hour had grown late and the house was silent, but even then, she couldn't make herself don her nightgown and descend the stairs to Spencer's bedroom.

Instead, she'd started cutting out leaves from paper to string across the ceiling of Evangeline's bedroom to add to the forestland aura.

Thankfully, the spare room upstairs had a writing table. Though it wasn't big and was somewhat rickety, it would suffice as a workstation when she needed the extra space. And it held the lantern that now glowed brightly in the dark of the night.

Paper cuttings littered the floor around the chair legs and under the table. But she had a variety of leaf types and sizes, all of which she'd paint tomorrow when Evangeline could help her.

She sat back in the chair and listened. The heavy

breathing from the next room told her the child was still asleep, as she'd been for the past couple of hours. Getting Evangeline to take a bath had been the most difficult of all the tasks Patience had faced with the little girl. Evangeline had given every possible excuse, even though she was filthier than a cowboy after a cattle drive.

Realizing the usual tactics wouldn't work with Evangeline, Patience suggested an enchanted bath filled with green water and green bubbles. Patience had concocted a mixture of soap with a little bit of green paint she had in her trunk. Then she'd added it to the bath water. Evangeline had been an eager participant after that. The trouble had been coaxing the child from the tub once the water had turned tepid and the bubbles had disappeared.

Finally, with the promise of a story about a princess who lived in an enchanted forest, Patience had managed to pluck the child from the tub. All the while she told the story, she'd helped Evangeline get ready for bed, even combing her hair and plaiting it. Once the child had been tucked under her covers, she hadn't stayed there—had kept making excuses to get out of bed to see what Patience was working on, until Patience had decided the best way to help Evangeline settle down was to do what Charity had done for her often as a child. She'd crawled into bed and held Evangeline's hand.

The trick had worked like magic. Evangeline had

gone to sleep and hadn't awoken since.

Patience smiled in contentment. No, Evangeline wasn't an easy or typical child. But Patience hadn't been either. In fact, she was sure she'd been much more difficult, if her mother's complaints were any indication.

She glanced at the twin bed, a stack of sheets and covers neatly folded on the end. Did she dare make up the bed and sleep in it tonight?

Her trunks crowded against the opposite wall where Spencer had deposited them after dinner. What would he say if she chose to sleep upstairs tonight rather than joining him?

Though he hadn't pressured her or said anything about the need to come down and sleep with him, she'd sensed his attraction. She wasn't sure how—maybe in the way he looked at her once in a while. Or maybe it was in the brief contacts he'd made at dinner, first grazing her back and then her arm. Both times she'd been sure he was making a point of some kind. But he'd remained silent.

The truth was, as hesitant as she was to join her husband in his bedroom and in his bed, she couldn't put it off forever. And if she refused to go down tonight, she might only frustrate him and cause tension between them.

No, it was for the best if she kept her end of the marriage bargain. She'd already frustrated him enough with her painting in Evangeline's room. Although she could tell that he'd tried to make the best of the situation for Evangeline's sake, he hadn't been able to hide his surprise or his consternation.

With a sigh, she set aside the scissors and the leaf she was cutting. Then before she could talk herself out of postponing her wifely duties any longer, she slipped into a simple summer nightgown, extinguished the lantern, and started down the steps.

Without a light, she made her way slowly and tried to be soundless. A part of her was hoping that maybe she could slide into the opposite side of the bed without waking him. If he remained asleep, then it wouldn't be her fault if they didn't have marital relations.

As she reached the bottom of the steps, she paused and drew in a breath. Her nerves were jittery again, and her pulse was racing.

What if he was still awake and waiting for her?

She closed her eyes and whispered a prayer for strength. Then she forced herself to keep going, tiptoeing as silently as an angel—at least, she hoped so. A second later, her fingers brushed against the doorway, and she was relieved to find it was open a crack. Carefully, to prevent any squealing, she inched it wider.

She let her eyes adjust to the moonlight streaming in through the open, curtainless window. She could see his outline in the center underneath a sheet, the heavy cover folded at the end of the bed.

He was a muscular man and took up most of the

space. There was no room for her. She'd return to the other bed and then, in the morning, explain that she'd come down but hadn't wanted to disturb him. He wouldn't be able to fault her for that, would he?

She almost expelled a relieved breath, but she held it in when he rolled so that he was facing away from her.

Had she awoken him?

Once again, she waited quietly, trying to discern what to do. Now that he'd shifted, there was enough space for her to slide into the bed. He still filled up most of the mattress, but she'd fit, especially if she hugged the edge and stayed as stiff as a corset.

Holding her breath, she crept to the bed. When she reached it, his presence was almost overwhelming and sent flutters through her stomach.

At least she liked him. That would make everything a little easier. Hopefully.

She hesitated before touching the mattress.

He didn't move, and his breathing continued at a steady pace.

Gingerly, she lowered herself until she was stretched out and as far from him as she could go without falling off. Six inches, if not more, separated her from Spencer. The proximity was close, but at least she wasn't rolling against him.

After several long moments, he shifted, almost as if he was giving her a couple more inches. But he was asleep, wasn't he?

With her head on the corner of the pillow, she stared through the darkness at the untextured and simple ceiling above. Her hands were fisted at her sides, her body rigid, and her toes suddenly cold. Did she dare try to cover herself with part of his blanket?

Though the August nights had remained warm recently, the temperatures could drop quickly. Maybe she could cover herself with the blanket on the end of the bed. She lay unmoving until the goosebumps forming on her bare arms made her shiver. Then, as carefully and slowly as before, she sat up, reached for the blanket, and pulled it over herself.

When she was finally lying back down and warm, she thought she heard Spencer exhale. But after she listened for a short while, her eyelids began to grow heavy. The past two days had been a whirlwind of change and a flurry of activity. And even though she wanted to slumber lightly and make sure she didn't disturb Spencer in any way, she was soon deeply asleep.

Spencer didn't dare move, hardly risked breathing.

Even though his body was motionless, his thoughts raced faster than a funnel cloud cutting a path through the prairie. A woman was in bed beside him. A beautiful woman who also was his wife. His lawfully wedded wife.

There was absolutely nothing untoward or even sinful about sleeping beside him. Because she was asleep. He knew that because he'd been conscious of her every movement and breath since the moment she'd pushed open the bedroom door.

The trouble was, he was wide awake. In fact, every single inch of his body was so fully awake that he was attuned to her like a bow to a fiddle. Even now, he was stretched tight with the need to turn over and just look at her. Just look, that's all.

But could he really stop with just the looking? After his reactions to her earlier in the evening, he doubted his self-control.

He'd hoped to deter her from coming closer to the bed when he'd rolled his back to her, thought maybe she'd get the hint that he didn't want to be disturbed. But clearly, she didn't catch on to subtlety very well. He thought he'd made it fairly obvious—without having to spell things out in embarrassing detail—that he wanted her to stay upstairs in the spare bedroom next to Evangeline.

Hadn't moving her trunks up to the room been statement enough that he was offering her separate sleeping arrangements?

He bit back a sigh. Apparently, it hadn't been.

And now . . . he had no choice but to spend the rest of the night with her.

What was she wearing? His mind formed the image of her in a nightdress, her shoulders bare except for thin straps. He'd easily be able to brush aside a flimsy strap with his thumb and at the same time graze the delicate length of her collarbone.

The room heated a hundred degrees at the fantasy. And in the next instant, he forced himself to think on something else. Like the way Evangeline had looked when he'd gone into her room to say goodnight. It had been late, but she'd been wide awake as usual. Only this time, her hair was damp from her bath and her skin smooth and pink and smelling like wildflowers.

Her eyes had been brighter than he'd ever seen them, and she'd been full of tales of her bath and the story Patience had told her. As he'd kissed her cheek, from the corner of his eye he'd caught Patience watching the interaction, a small smile hovering over her lips.

He'd wanted to smile his relief that Evangeline hadn't scared her away yet. And he'd wanted to thank her for managing to get Evangeline to do things—like take a bath—that the best nursemaids hadn't been able to accomplish.

But as soon as he'd risen from Evangeline's bedside, Patience had slipped away and disappeared into the spare room. A moment later, on his way down the hallway, he'd halted in front of her doorway. She'd turned questioning eyes upon him, and the tenderness in them had made his stomach topple off a precipice.

But Evangeline had followed him and wanted another hug and kiss. Patience had allowed the girl an extra moment of affection but then had ushered her back to bed. He'd waited in the hallway for a minute, listening to her soft-spoken and patient way of interacting with Evangeline, not a trace of irritation in her tone.

After he'd returned to the kitchen and his chair near the stove where he usually studied the ranch ledgers and correspondences from various vendors, Evangeline's soft thumping and getting out of bed happened several times before Patience had somehow brought it to an end, all without tears and tantrums, and the little girl had gone to sleep.

The painting in Evangeline's room, the colorful bath, even the bedtime stories, seemed to be occupying his daughter. But how long would Patience be able to engage Evangeline with such methods before the child was back to her usual wild ways?

And once that happened, would Patience want to leave? Would she reach her limit just like all the other caretakers?

Spencer released another taut breath, still facing the wall and open window. Just because they were married didn't mean everything would go better than with a nursemaid. In fact, things could actually go much worse. Evangeline had a tender heart. She'd be brokenhearted if

Patience ever decided to leave.

Would it be better if Evangeline didn't form so tight a connection until they were certain Patience would stay? He'd already made the resolve for himself. But how could he hold Evangeline back?

The truth was, he'd never been proficient at restraining Evangeline. And so rather than trying and likely failing, maybe he had to simply ensure that Patience didn't want to leave him. Didn't ever have reason to let her mind wander to another man.

But what could he do to ensure that?

Her soft, even exhalations came from behind him, but she remained motionless, quiet, unassuming. She likely didn't expect much in return from him. In fact, by coming to his bed, she was even telling him that she was willing to do what was expected of her as a wife without compulsion on his part.

Should he take up her offer? All he had to do was roll over and reach for her. He'd gone so long without a woman, and now that he had one in his bed, his needs were too keen for him to ignore.

Maybe those needs had once been extinct. Maybe. But now, with only one day of marriage, they'd been excavated. In fact, they'd risen from the dead and were a dozen times stronger than ever, almost as if they'd gained power while lying in the grave.

If only she weren't so achingly sweet and gloriously

beautiful. But she was . . . and he'd relish exploring every inch of her.

He shifted, almost turned, then stopped himself.

Devil it. Doing so would be selfish on his part. And he couldn't forget all the reasons why he needed to go slowly with this marriage and do things right, couldn't forget that he hadn't wanted to get remarried, couldn't forget how quickly things could change and come crashing to an end.

He pinched his eyes closed and drew in a breath. For now, he was sticking to his resolution to keep his relationship with Patience platonic.

He let his shoulders relax, trying to ease the tension there. In the morning, he had to be more direct with her and let her know that they could wait to be together. He wasn't sure what explanation he'd give to her. But he had to assure her that they had no need to rush anything.

In the meantime, he'd be on his best behavior. He'd work on showing her he could be a good husband. He could certainly figure out ways to win her over, couldn't he?

9

Patience stirred. A feeling that she wasn't alone awoke her.

Even before she opened her eyes, her senses came to life. The softness of sheets, the cool air against her nose, the warmth of a blanket surrounding her, the daylight chasing away the darkness of night.

Wakefulness never came easily for Patience. She tended to linger longer in bed than her sisters. And this morning was one of those times when she wanted to loiter and savor all the events of the previous day—when she'd gotten married to Spencer Wolcott, the strong and handsome Englishman with the saddest but most captivating eyes.

She snuggled deeper under the blanket, molded her face to the pillow, and took a deep breath.

At the creak of the mattress beside her, she froze, and her eyes flew open. In the same instant, the rush of memories from late last night came running back. She'd crept downstairs and crawled into bed with Spencer. He'd already been asleep and hadn't awakened—thankfully—at her approach.

But now?

He was facing her, his head resting on his arm. His eyes were open, and he was looking directly at her. The daylight had indeed come, turning his eyes into an enchanted forest, just like the one she was painting on Evangeline's wall. His dark brown hair was mussed from sleep, but it only made him look younger and more appealing.

How long had he been awake and watching her sleep?

The very thought sent a strange hop of anticipation through her stomach. They hadn't done anything last night. Would he expect something now? Did married couples share intimacy during daylight hours? Or was it reserved for under the cover of darkness?

His eyes, though still framed by his dark slanted brows, seemed to be caressing each inch of her cheek and chin.

Her heart quivered with a strange need for his fingers to follow the path of his eyes.

As though reading the suggestion in her expression, his gaze slid to her mouth.

Was he ready to kiss her? Was that how this would start? Did she want it to start? Her first kiss.

She took him in more fully, the sheet covering him but not able to hide the fact that he wasn't wearing a shirt, that his bare chest showed partially from his arms up—a smooth chest sculpted with muscles that looked as hard as granite, that practically begged her to dig her fingers in and scale them.

Embarrassment swelled within her. What was she thinking? How could she be so wanton? What if he didn't have a stitch of clothing on underneath the sheet? And why would he? Especially if he'd been waiting for her last night.

Her body flushed with strange heat. Oh, goodness gracious. She needed to get out of the bed. Perhaps she'd been too hasty in joining him there and should have stayed in the little room upstairs.

She lifted her head and started to push up. Wasn't it time to check on Evangeline anyway?

His eyes widened, as though sensing her growing panic. "Wait," he whispered.

She froze. This was it. She swallowed her trepidation and slowly lowered herself back to the pillow. What would he do first?

She held herself stiff.

Instead of moving toward her, he leaned slightly away. "You were good with Evangeline yesterday."

"I was?"

"Very much so."

She relaxed against the pillow. "She was an enthusiastic and willing accomplice to all my fanciful ideas."

"Probably because she is so fanciful herself."

"Yes, I can see that." Patience couldn't keep from smiling.

Spencer's lips curved into a tender smile of his own. The dark stubble on his chin and jaw contrasted the show of his white teeth. And the early morning light was soft and subtle, making his smile truly beautiful.

"If I had a camera, I'd capture your smile in a photograph." The words came out before she could filter them. Immediately she shifted her gaze, mortified with herself for her forwardness.

He was silent. Was he thinking what a ninny she was?

"I should like to capture your smile too."

At the sincerity of his tone, she lifted her lashes. Was he being serious?

His smile was gone, but his expression remained gentle and even encouraging. "Have you ever had a photograph taken? I hear the process is complicated, especially the development."

"I've never been photographed, though I admit to tinkering around with a camera when a photographer left his unattended this past Fourth of July celebration."

Spencer's smile made a slight appearance again. "You didn't."

"I did. And I may or may not have taken some pictures of the events."

His smile widened, sending light bubbles of happiness floating through her stomach.

"How about you?" she asked. "Have you ever had a photograph?"

"Once with my family." For a few minutes, he told her about his family in England, that he'd grown up near Norwich and had an older brother who resided on the family's estate with his wife and several children. Before moving, Spencer had lived in Norwich, too, and managed his father's properties. He'd visited his father's investment in Colorado four years ago, shortly after Evangeline's birth. "I loved the wildness of this place," he whispered. "So after my wife died, I decided to come back."

His wife. He hadn't spoken of her yet. And neither had Evangeline, likely too young to remember her mother.

A shadow fell across his face, and he stared at the empty space in the bed between them. Was he thinking about the past? Should she ask about his loss? Or should she wait and let him talk about everything when he was ready to do so?

His brows fell into a deeper slant. Was that loss why he was so sad most of the time? He was obviously still grieving, had probably loved his wife deeply and had run away from the memories of her in England to start a new life here in America.

"Will you ever return to England?" She asked what she hoped was a safe question, one that didn't pry too deeply into his hurts.

He shook his head. "Perhaps I shall one day visit. But I have no wish to return permanently."

"Then you love the ranch?"

"It's demanding but satisfying nonetheless."

His bare arm flexed beneath his cheek, reminding her again that he was bare-chested, that only covers separated them from complete indecency.

"Father Zieber says the ranchers are concerned that you're accumulating the smaller ranches in the area and becoming too big." Once the words were out, she realized just how unflattering and accusatory they sounded. Why was she bringing the subject up, anyway? If only she had more social graces. "Not that you're actually doing so—"

"I am buying up the smaller ranches and expanding my operations." His voice was calm, as though he was accustomed to the accusations and having to defend himself. "But I'm not bent on destroying anyone."

"I didn't think so. You seem too kind to deliberately hurt someone."

"Too kind?" His brows quirked.

Was he offended, amused, or enamored with her description of him? If only she were better at understanding cues. All she could do was explain herself more. "I haven't had to live here long to see that your workers admire and respect you. They wouldn't show such loyalty to a man who wasn't kind."

"Would they show loyalty to a man who pays them well?"

"Perhaps. But not for long."

"Then kindness is the key to commanding loyalty?" His question was suddenly so serious she had the distinct feeling they were no longer speaking about the workers. But as before, she didn't understand enough to figure out what else he might be referring to.

"When you are kind, you don't need to command loyalty. It will be freely given."

He didn't respond. Instead, he studied her intently, almost as though he was attempting to see beneath the surface of her words and find out if she held any ulterior motives. He didn't need to worry. She didn't know how to play any games with men. She was who she was, often to a fault.

His gaze made another circuit around her face, causing the bubbles inside to fizzle and float again. She'd never had a man look at her so intensely. What did it mean?

As if sensing her question, he dropped his attention back to the sheet. "I've told you about my family. Now tell me about yours."

She appreciated that he was making an effort to learn

more about her. She shared with him about her family's break with their Quaker community and how then, not long after that, her parents had died of influenza. She and her sisters had tried to survive on their own but hadn't been able to make it, had lost their home and their father's woodworking shop. They'd reached out to family and former friends in their old Quaker church, but no one had come to their aid. When they'd received the notice of the inheritance from Uncle John's solicitor, they'd had little choice but to move west.

"Charity and I both considered getting married in order to stay. But Charity wanted more for us than marriages of convenience."

"Then am I correct in assuming that, similar to Felicity, she will not rejoice in your arranged union to me?"

Patience hesitated in her response. Charity would be frustrated. "Hopefully, under the circumstances, my sister will understand."

He was silent for a moment. "This cousin. Is she really your uncle's daughter?"

"I believe so. But Felicity doesn't like how everything came about. She wonders why our cousin is just now coming forward, so soon after the gold was found on my uncle's property."

"Perhaps she is a fraud."

"She has the family Bible and letters. And of course,

the family red hair."

He gave a slight shrug, one that only highlighted the rippling muscles in his bare shoulder. "I don't think it hurts to question her authenticity."

"It's possible she heard about the debt my uncle had and held back from coming earlier because she didn't want to become saddled with it the same way we were. But now that it's no longer an obstacle, she decided to claim what rightfully belongs to her."

"What was this debt?"

For a few minutes, she gave him the shortened version about how they'd almost lost their homestead earlier in the summer because they'd owed the bank money. Their situation had been dire then too.

Spencer was so relaxed against his pillow—his expression, his eyes, even his brows were peaceful. The scruff on his face made him look rugged and entirely too appealing. But there was also something gentlemanly about his bearing that apparently he couldn't shake.

"I almost accepted Bart Kruger's marriage proposal then."

"The tanner?" Spencer's tone held a scoffing note. "That stuffy old man?"

"He's a nice fellow."

Again, Spencer scoffed. "You're too beautiful and young for a man like him."

She paused, trying to digest Spencer's compliment.

"Beautiful? Do you think so?"

He didn't answer her. Instead, his gaze flitted over her body, tucked away underneath the cover. He couldn't see anything, not even the tiniest part of her nightgown. But his eyes lit with appreciation anyway, an appreciation that sent a shiver of anticipation through her. Anticipation for what, she didn't know. But she did know she hadn't minded spending the night with him, that it hadn't been nearly as bad as she'd thought it would be.

The room around them was getting lighter as sunlight streamed in through the window. Even though the calls of ranch hands and the bellow of steers came from the direction of the barns, the morning was still mostly silent. And the house was exceptionally so. Not a sound anywhere except their conversation.

Spencer lifted his hand and combed his hair back from his forehead but still rested his head on the pillow beside hers.

She was strangely warmed by the time with him, whispering together in bed. It wasn't anything she'd ever expected to do with him. But she liked it, could imagine many more mornings waking up like this and talking together before starting their days. At least, she hoped they would have many such mornings.

As he finished combing through the messy strands, the sheet slipped off his arm, revealing more of his bare chest. And even though she didn't want to stare at the broad expanse, she couldn't stop herself. The bulging muscles were so well defined she could almost believe he was a Renaissance sculpture crafted by a master artist.

What she wouldn't give to run her fingers over so fine a piece of craftsmanship. But she held herself back, trying to content herself with merely admiring him.

After a lengthy silence, she glanced up to find that he was watching her watching him. And his eyes had turned a dark green-brown, like thick and tangled branches, pulling her in so that she couldn't pry herself loose even if she'd wanted to.

The air seemed to shift, and her breath felt tight in her chest. What was happening now? Was this part of the intimacy of sharing a bed? This awakening desire?

He didn't move toward her. Instead, he swallowed hard, rolled to his back, and closed his eyes. "It would be best if we waited to share the bed again"—his voice was strained—"until we have the chance to get to know each other better."

She looked away from him, too embarrassed to add to the conversation. At the same time, she tried to make sense of what he was telling her.

"You can sleep in the room upstairs." His whisper was taut, just like her chest.

Was that why he'd moved her things up there to begin with? Because he'd expected her to sleep there too? A wave of mortification rushed in. She should have realized he hadn't wanted her in his room. But she'd misunderstood and made a fool out of herself by coming down and crawling into bed with him.

She was such a dolt. What must he think of her? That she was too forward, too eager? Maybe he was distressed at the thought of being with another woman—any other woman—besides his wife.

It was her turn to roll to her back and close her eyes. Even with her eyes shut, her mistake glared at her. "I'm sorry—"

A dainty body launched onto the bed. "Mama and Papa!" Still in her nightgown, Evangeline crawled toward them, a happy smile lighting her sleepy face.

Patience sat up and held her arms open to the girl, her heart already full of love toward the little one after only a day of being a mother. As Evangeline eagerly fell against her, Patience wrapped her up and kissed her head.

Over Evangeline's head, she caught Spencer gazing at them, his brows slanted in that sad way of his. Was he thinking about Evangeline's real mother and all that she'd lost in being unable to see Evangeline grow up?

Without saying anything more, Spencer pushed himself up, dragging the sheet with him. He grabbed his clothes, neatly draped over the bedside chair, and then stalked from the room without a glance back.

She might not be proficient in picking up on clues. But in this case, Spencer had just made it mighty clear that he wasn't interested in her as a wife and only wanted her to be Evangeline's mother. She ought to be relieved. Instead, she was strangely disappointed.

10

Spencer laid a hand on the swollen abdomen of the dead steer.

Nearby, Buck knelt beside another dead steer. Several other ranch hands had ridden out to the west pasture with them and were down scouring the ground and trying to figure out what had happened.

There wasn't much daylight left for investigating. The western sky was golden with the setting sun, which was dropping behind Mosquito Range, lighting up the sprawling rocky peaks that rose above the tree line.

Spencer stood and swept his gaze over the dead cattle sprawled out over the pasture, frustration churning in his gut. He tallied the number of deaths. Twenty-six. With so many dead, it wasn't an accident. Someone had poisoned his steers intentionally. That was the only explanation.

Thank the Lord in heaven above that only this stray group had been targeted and not one of the larger herds.

And thank the Lord one of his men had spotted the dead cattle while delivering salt licks.

Buck straightened, a scowl marring his features. "Who do you think did the dirty deed?"

Spencer's mind ticked through the possibilities. Unfortunately, his list of enemies was growing longer with every passing day, especially with his increased efforts to fence in his property with the barbed wire.

But if he had to point a finger, he'd aim it at one of the three smaller ranches with land adjacent to his. Stirrup Ranch was in the most financial trouble, so much so that Spencer had gone out and visited the owner last week and offered to buy the place.

Yes, he was still relying upon his father's investment for expansion. Soon enough, he would be able to buy out his father's partner and eventually even his father. With the price of beef soaring, he was hoping to command a premium of sixty dollars a head, the highest since the War of Rebellion more than ten years ago. Someday, he'd be turning enough profit to own the ranch without financial backing from anyone else.

Of course, anything could go wrong in ranching. Droughts, insects, disease, and even wild animals could cut into profit margins. But by producing his own hay and selling that too, he'd added another source of revenue.

Buck rested his hand on his revolver, the hardness in

his expression saying what words didn't—that he was ready for a fight. "If I had to put my bet on who it was, I reckon it's those fellas over at Stirrup Ranch. They're always pawing and bellering about something."

Spencer didn't want a fight, but he might not have a choice. Regardless, he had to take more precautions. "We'll have to keep watch around the clock from now on." It would make him short-staffed for the haying, but he couldn't afford to lose more of his cattle.

One of the cowhands standing near a gopher mound gave a shout and held up a handful of weeds. "Got ourselves the cause of the poisoning."

Spencer didn't have to go closer to know what the fellow had found. The height of the plant as well as the few remaining bluish-purple flowers told him what it was. Wild larkspur. Though sheep could eat the plant without harm, if cows or horses ate even a small amount, they would have convulsions and die.

That was why he and his men made sure none of the larkspur grew anywhere on the ranch. Which meant that if his cows had eaten it, someone had deliberately fed it to them. Or worse yet, the culprits had spread it around in various places. If that were the case, not only were the remaining cattle still in danger, but by next spring, the plant would start sprouting up all over the ranch.

Spencer blew out a tight breath. Tomorrow, before starting haying, they would have to scour hundreds of acres for larkspur and try to find every last piece. They couldn't let a single blade remain.

First, they had to dispose of the poisoned cattle.

Spencer started toward where they'd left their mounts a safe distance from the cattle. "I'll head back and send out more men to help with the fires."

"You ain't staying?" Buck's question was tinged with surprise.

"Not tonight." Spencer didn't slow his stride. He always worked right alongside his ranch hands. In fact, he was usually the first to do any task and the last to leave. But for today, he was done. He was hungry and tired.

And anxiety had been tugging at him all day.

He hadn't wanted to worry about Patience and how she was faring with Evangeline, but thoughts of them hadn't been far from his mind. Yes, Patience and Evangeline had gotten along well yesterday. But that was because everything was new, Evangeline was still enamored with Patience, and she hadn't yet done anything major to test Patience.

But sooner or later the novelty would wear off, and Evangeline would misbehave.

If it wasn't Evangeline driving Patience away, what if something else did? What if he did something she didn't like and she decided to find another man to make her happy?

As he reached his horse, he drew in a breath of the hot

dusty air and told himself everything would be alright, that he was worrying for nothing. But that was what he'd first thought with Honora, and how wrong he'd been.

"Shucks!" Buck's comment rang out, laced with mirth. "Forgot about your pretty new filly. Reckon she's got you on a short rein."

The other ranch hands guffawed.

But something in his foreman's tone pricked against Spencer like a rusty piece of barbed wire.

"If she was mine, I'd be just as eager to get home and . . ." The rest of Buck's comment was vulgar.

Spencer stiffened, low-burning fury striking to life in his gut.

He supposed Buck was only stating—albeit inappropriately—what everyone else was thinking. It was only natural they'd assume he was enjoying the pleasures to be found with so beautiful a woman.

But he didn't want anyone thinking about Patience in that manner. Not now and not anytime in the future.

The laughter of the other men had faded. And as he pivoted slowly, they dropped their gazes, because no doubt his expression was as stormy as a towering thundercloud. He never yelled. He was too much of a gentleman to do so. But sometimes he wished he could break past the barriers inside himself and let his emotions out.

"Mind your tongue." The clipped voice was about as

irritated as he allowed himself. "And henceforth, you may refer to my wife as Mrs. Wolcott. Do I make myself clear?"

Buck's smile disappeared. And though his expression wasn't contrite, he nodded.

Without waiting for another comment or question, Spencer mounted and started across the open plain toward the ranch house. As he rode, there was a small part of him that wished he were going home to a real marriage, that he could have Patience in his bed again tonight, and that this time he wouldn't roll away from her but would instead wrap his arms around her, pull her close, and kiss a trail around her face until he ended up at her mouth, where he'd lose himself.

Just the thought of doing so turned him inside out and upside down, the blood rushing to his head and making him dizzy. Yes, they'd only talked. And yes, the talking had been surprisingly nice.

But all the while they'd been talking, he'd been thinking that she was only wearing a nightgown underneath the blanket—a very thin, silky nightgown and a very thin, soft blanket. And he'd been thinking about how pretty her features were, how curvy her body was, and how she was only inches away from him. Along with the fact that she'd crawled into bed with him without any coercing or manipulating or pleading.

Had she wanted to be with him? Or had she simply

been doing what any new wife would have?

No doubt it was the latter. And no doubt he'd confused her by insisting that she sleep in the spare bedroom.

With a sigh, he kicked his horse faster. If only he could put his past behind him and learn to trust again. Not every woman was like Honora. In fact, Patience—other than her beauty—was nothing like Honora, especially in how she treated Evangeline.

Honora had never warmed up to their daughter, had preferred to allow the nursemaid to take care of the baby. Of course, Spencer couldn't be too harsh on Honora's mothering skills. After all, many among the highborn and wealthy classes relied upon others to raise their children.

Regardless, he liked the way Patience interacted with Evangeline. He could only pray the goodwill would continue.

As the quaint old house came into view, he could see that Patience and Evangeline were outside at the front. He wanted to veer his horse immediately toward them. But he forced himself to ride to the barn first, dispensed instructions regarding the poisoned cattle, prepared a plan with Tex for guard duty, and then discussed how to conduct a thorough search over the rest of the property first thing in the morning.

By the time he strode through the ranch yard toward the house, the sun had fallen behind the western range completely. Only faint light remained, and the first star of the night had made an appearance overhead.

Even so, Patience and Evangeline were still outside, kneeling side by side in the grass, bent low to the ground, peering underneath the porch, a lantern on the porch rail casting a long glow over them.

As he stopped above them, Evangeline was the first to notice his presence. "Papa!" She scrambled up and threw her arms around his legs in a tight hug.

"Hello, darling." He placed a hand upon her head to find that her hair was neatly parted down the center and plaited into two braids with ribbons tied up and down each one. It was slightly flamboyant, but who was he to complain about an abundance of ribbon if that had helped Patience convince Evangeline into letting her manage her hair?

Patience gave one last lingering look underneath the porch before pushing up until she was standing before him. Though she was wearing a simpler skirt and blouse today than yesterday, somehow she appeared just as vibrant, especially because her cheeks were rosy and her blue eyes sparkled with life.

She offered him a tentative smile, her uncertainty about how to approach him and their marriage hanging in the air around her.

Since he'd been the one to institute the boundary, perhaps he needed to also be the one to set an example to her on how they could get along.

"How was your day?" he asked, this time taking in the splotch of paint on her cheek, the smudge of dirt on her nose, and the cobwebs sticking to her braid.

"It was lovely." Her voice rang with such sincerity that he could almost believe she was telling him the truth. Why was it so difficult to accept that Patience might actually enjoy being with Evangeline?

Evangeline pulled back. "We found baby bunnies under the porch, Papa."

"I'll have one of the ranch hands clear them out later."

"No!" Both Evangeline and Patience cried their objection at the same time. Then Evangeline explained how the bunnies were a family and belonged together and rattled off the names they'd given the creatures. After that, Evangeline was eager to show him the wind chimes they'd created to hang from the porch rafter, the colorful pillow they'd added to the porch swing, and the flower gardens they'd formed on either side of the porch steps with smooth stones framing them in.

"They won't have flowers until the spring." Evangeline ran a hand over the cleared spot. "And Mama said that I get to help her do the planting."

Patience tucked a loose strand of hair behind her ear, revealing fingers stained with paint and soil. "I'm sorry again today that I didn't ask you first. I tend to get carried away with projects. Then one thing leads to another, and before I realize it, I'm doing more than I should."

"You've no need to apologize." He supposed he'd grown accustomed to denying himself any pleasure or comforts or beauty, so that now he wasn't quite sure how to allow it back into his life.

"Next time, I'll try to remember to ask—"

"This is your home now too. You may do as you wish."

Evangeline was watching the interaction with wide eyes. Was he being kind enough to Patience? Maybe he needed to do more.

"Are you sure?" Patience asked. "I can be more careful—"

He lifted a hand to her cheek and gently caressed along the line of her jaw, cutting off her words and silencing her. She didn't pull away, and in fact, even seemed to incline her head into his touch.

Her eyes locked with his, the blue bright and curious. And welcoming?

He slid his fingers to her chin, relishing the smoothness of her skin and the perfection of her features.

Her gaze didn't budge from his and only seemed to give him permission to do more.

More? Flint sparked against flint inside him, and the conversation they'd just been having fled from his mind. Instead, all he could think about was how the lantern light was turning the wisps of her hair into gold.

From the corner of his eyes, he could see the cook's assistant carrying a basket toward the kitchen door, and his stomach chose that moment to rumble.

"Shall we have our supper?" He let his hand fall away from her face. He couldn't do more with Patience. He wasn't ready for more.

Evangeline reached for his hand and grasped Patience's and began to tug them toward the dining hall.

He resisted, standing his ground. "We're eating in our kitchen tonight."

Evangeline halted her efforts. "Why, Papa?"

"Because we're a family now, and we should have a life separate from the workers."

Evangeline cocked her head, clearly trying to decide if she liked the new arrangement or whether she should protest. Instead of doing either, she turned her sights upon Patience as though to take her cue from her new mama.

Patience gave him a gracious smile and nod. "I like the prospect of an evening together, don't you, Evangeline?"

Evangeline hesitated.

"Perhaps after the meal we can show your papa how to play the new ribbons and buttons game we made."

The child finally nodded, and her expression filled with hope. "Would you like that, Papa?"

"Of course I would."

She clapped her hands and twirled, her happiness brightening up the dusk. How could such a small offer mean so much?

Without another moment of hesitation, Evangeline began to tug them again, this time toward the front door. As they tromped up the steps, he leaned toward Patience and whispered, "How do you do it?"

"Do what?" she whispered back.

"Get her to do your bidding?"

Patience glanced down at the girl with affection. "I don't always succeed, but I prefer gentle guidance over condemnation and criticism."

Spencer didn't know exactly what that meant, but he liked the sound of it nonetheless.

As they entered the house and made their way into the kitchen, the cook's assistant was in the process of placing the food onto the table. Once he finished and took his leave, Patience bustled about, setting the table and attempting to dish up the food.

The kitchen was a small room, hardly big enough for the simple round oak table with four matching chairs along with a sink and medium-sized cast iron stove along one wall and the floor-to-ceiling cupboard that lined the other.

As she passed by, Spencer captured her arm and halted her. She glanced first at his hand on her arm, her eyes widening, before lifting her gaze to his. The blue was like the sky right after sunset with a few stars starting to glimmer expectantly.

Had he overstepped himself in touching her? He hadn't meant to.

"Please, sit down." He released her and motioned to the chair next to Evangeline's. "You're not a servant. You are my wife."

She hesitated with her hand on the serving spoon. "I don't mind. My sisters and I did everything for ourselves."

"Next time I go to town, I shall hire a housekeeper." He'd had a housekeeper when he'd first arrived, the wife of one of the older ranch hands. But after she'd passed away, he hadn't hired anyone new, had instead relied heavily upon the nursemaids for daily tasks.

"I really don't mind." Her cheeks flushed.

"And I do mind. I want you to be free to attend to Evangeline and pursue whatever makes you happy without worry of menial tasks."

Though she didn't smile, pleasure brightened her face. "Thank you."

He couldn't take his eyes from her. Didn't want to. Instead, he wanted to look at her all evening long and get his fill before the long days of haying—although he suspected that with a woman like Patience, he'd never get his fill and would always crave more of her.

11

Patience was determined to be in the kitchen before Spencer on the first day of haying. But as her eyes flew open in the dark of the early morning, she suspected she'd failed in her mission.

Without bothering to get dressed or coil her hair, she rolled out of bed, slipped into her robe, and started down the stairs in her bare feet. At the sight of faint light coming from under Spencer's closed door and the darkness of the kitchen, she allowed herself a victorious smile.

As she stepped onto the cold floorboards of the hallway, his bedroom door swung open, and the light poured out over her.

She took a rapid step back toward the stairs. What if he didn't want her to see him off?

"Everything okay?" He peered down the hallway and then to the stairway behind her. His brown hair was still uncombed and fell in roguish waves that made her fingers curl with the need to brush them back.

Thankfully he was fully attired and was just finishing buttoning his shirt. Even so, as his strong fingers worked to close his shirt, she glanced toward the kitchen, his act of dressing too intimate to watch. "I know you're in a rush to get going this morning, so I wanted to help with the coffee."

"Thank you. That's very kind of you." His reply sounded formal, as if she'd offered to make him a three-course meal instead of a simple pot of coffee, although the previous evening he'd made it clear that he didn't expect her to cook his meals or do *menial tasks*. Someone of his class would expect a housekeeper and not a wife to do the work. As lovely as the sentiment was, she couldn't fathom being waited on like that and spending the majority of her time in leisure.

She waited a moment, not sure if she should pass by or if she should wait for him to say more. When he didn't offer another comment and instead stared at her, his eyes widening and darkening as he took her in from her loose hair to her bare feet, she glanced down at herself to realize she hadn't closed her robe all the way, and her nightgown was visible underneath. Even though it was a plain and unadorned garment, as was the custom among Quakers, it was still thin and revealing.

And was the outline of her bare body underneath

visible in the glow of the lantern light?

With heat rushing into her face, she fumbled with the robe, flapping the ends together. In the same motion, she darted toward the kitchen, needing to put some distance between herself and Spencer.

As she slipped into the room, she paused and leaned against the wall next to the white enamel standing sink. She pressed a hand against her strangely fluttering chest. His caress against her face last night had never been far from her mind, nor had the way he'd touched her arm when he'd wanted her to sit down at the table. She'd liked the contact in both instances so much that she'd almost not wanted him to pull away from her.

What was happening to her? Were these feelings normal for a husband and wife?

At the sounds coming from his bedroom, she knew she couldn't dawdle over such thoughts, not when she was already spending too much time thinking about him. She straightened and started toward the lantern that sat in the middle of the table with the match canister beside it. In no time she had the lantern lit, the coffee ground, and the pot bubbling on the stove.

Even though she'd only been at the ranch a few days, she'd already begun to make plans for how to paint and decorate each room. And the kitchen was no exception. It didn't have a stitch of color, not even curtains in the windows. Someday soon, though, she would paint the walls a pale green and accent with white and brown. The color scheme seemed like one that Spencer would approve of. And of course, it reminded her of the color of his eyes.

Although the table was small and likely meant to be a worktable, the chairs around it made it a cozy place to congregate. She imagined it was especially comfortable in the winter with the stove pumping out heat.

When Spencer made his appearance a moment later, she only had to glimpse him in all his rugged cowboy glory for warmth to start pumping through her just like the stove. Though she wanted to fan her face, she made herself pour coffee into a mug. As she did so, she could feel him in the kitchen behind her, scraping a chair out and sitting down, his presence as overpowering as always.

With the mug in hand, she hesitated to turn around and face him and whatever was growing between them. But as the heat of the mug began to burn her flesh, she inwardly chastised herself. She was being too sensitive and needed to approach him as she would any other person she met—with both kindness and concern.

She made herself pivot, walk to him calmly, and place the coffee on the table in front of him.

In the process of unholstering his gun, he paused. "Thank you, Patience."

"Would you like me to make you breakfast as well. I may not be a good cook like Felicity, but I am proficient enough to make toast and eggs."

"I shall go eat something with the men in the dining hall before heading out to the field." He lifted the cup to his lips and took a long slurp. His hair was now combed and slicked back neatly, but the dark scruff on his jaw and chin remained.

"I don't mind." She guessed if he asked her to scale the highest peak in Colorado at this point, she probably would.

He'd clicked open the cylinder on his pistol and began adding ammunition. "I meant what I said last night. I do not expect you to be my servant. You're my wife."

"You work long days with your men. The least I can do is take care of you when you're home."

He took another sip, his pupils large and dark in the shadows of predawn. But his eyes fixed upon her with such intensity that she could feel the searing sensation down to her toes.

Her knees growing weak—an increasingly common condition whenever he was near—she pulled out the chair across from him and sat before she collapsed. He probably didn't have too long before he needed to head out. But a few minutes of sitting together and talking would surely be okay, wouldn't it? Especially because, from the lack of footsteps overhead, Evangeline was still asleep.

He slid in the last bullet and closed the cylinder. "I have heard Quakers were abolitionists in your War

Between the States. Do the Quakers also not believe in having servants?"

"Wealthy Quakers do have servants. But my father was a woodworker. While we always had everything we needed and more, we couldn't afford to hire anyone. And we didn't mind doing the work."

He was silent, as though digesting her answer. She liked that about him—that he wasn't self-absorbed and was a good listener. "Now, after my time in Colorado, I understand the benefit of laboring for oneself instead of relying upon a servant."

"Yes, I suppose you feel a greater sense of independence here."

While he sipped his coffee, he spoke of growing up with wealth and privilege and what a shock it had been for him during his first trip to America, but how he'd adjusted.

She'd refilled his coffee already and finally poured herself a cup at his insistence. She took a sip, the warmth sliding through her. "Evangeline mentioned that her mother died when she was but an infant of two. Does that mean your wife was able to be here with you on your first trip?"

He grew suddenly still and silent.

Had she overstepped in asking about his first wife?

His brows slanted and his forehead furrowed like the beginning of a storm forming over a mountain peak.

Yes, she'd pried too far. The warmth of the room, the comfortable conversation, and the waft of coffee in the air had lulled her into too much familiarity with him.

He pushed aside his mug and stood. Then he swiped up his gun, stuffed it in his holster, and started toward the door with rapid strides.

"I'm sorry." She jumped up so quickly that her coffee sloshed over the rim of her mug. "I was insensitive to ask about your last wife when you're clearly still grieving."

By the door and in the process of swiping his hat from a hook on the wall, he froze.

Had she said something wrong once more? Maybe she simply needed to refrain from mentioning her at all.

"I'm not grieving." His words came out stiffly.

"Oh." It had been two years. That was long enough for many people to move on and find healing from the loss of a loved one. Or was he implying that he'd never grieved? That maybe parting ways with his wife hadn't been difficult?

He was quiet, gripping his hat hard. Then he settled it on his head. "Thank you again for the coffee." And with that, he opened the door and left.

The darkness of dawn still lingered, broken now by faint light, enough that she could see him stalking across the yard. Regardless of what his feelings—or lack of them—had been for his previous wife, a strange need swelled within her to find a way to gain more of his affection.

She held out her hand and looked at her wedding ring, as she'd done many times since the morning he'd placed it on her finger. Even though she'd never expected a man to truly want her, he had chosen her. That had to count for something.

Maybe if she were steadfast and loving, he'd overlook her faults and learn to care about her in return. She didn't want to let her expectations rise too high. But was it possible she could someday share with her husband the same passion that Charity had with Hudson? Oh, such passion.

At the image of the newlywed couple kissing with an ardor that had been almost shocking, an intense longing squeezed Patience, making her suddenly breathless.

She didn't expect that with Spencer. But she had to admit, now that she was married, she wanted it more than she'd thought she would.

12

She'd been a mother for almost six days.

Patience squeezed Evangeline's hand in hers as they entered Simpkins General Store. The waft of kerosene, leather, and ripe cheese greeted them.

"Can I get candy, Mama?" Evangeline peered eagerly at the counter that contained glass jars of various shapes and sizes filled with peppermint sticks, licorice, lemon drops, and rock candy.

Patience's gaze bypassed the counters and landed on the shelves overflowing with canned vegetables, spices, fabric, sewing notions, soaps, cartridges . . . and paints, paper, glue, dye, and all the other items she'd requested the store have available. For her. And her artwork.

That was when they'd had their uncle's gold and an endless supply of money. Now . . . she had nothing, not even a penny to replenish what she was running low on.

Of course, she had Spencer's account. He'd indicated

that she could purchase anything she needed.

But she couldn't buy things for herself. She didn't feel right about that. Even so, with all the decorating and painting she was doing in and around the house, she would soon run out. And then what would she do?

She gave a shake of her head, as much to deny herself as Evangeline. "First we need to get our supplies for the surprise."

"Oh, yes." Evangeline broke free from Patience, clapped her hands, and twirled in a circle.

Several men in chairs around a checkerboard positioned on an empty keg paused their conversation. Taking puffs on their pipes, their gazes shifted to the opposite end of the store to another counter before swinging back to Patience expectantly.

Patience had the feeling she was on display, and as soon as she took in the couple at the far counter, she realized why.

It was her cousin Lizette and her husband Gage, and they seemed to be in the process of buying half the store, if the stack of items on the counter was any indication. Of course, they now had all the Courtney gold and unlimited access to the bank account and could purchase anything they wanted.

Lizette was attired in another fancy gown similar in style to the one she'd been wearing the first time Patience had met her. It wasn't elegant or stylish like those Charity had left for her and Felicity. Instead, the gowns appeared older, brighter, gaudier, like a fake gemstone next to real jewels.

Lizette was watching Patience warily, the same way she had the day she'd arrived at the homestead.

Disappointment pricked at Patience. She wanted to have an amiable relationship with Lizette. After all, the young woman was family. But from the moment she'd met Lizette and Gage, they'd exuded an aloofness, even animosity, that seemed to push everyone away.

When Patience had talked with Felicity about it, she'd come to the conclusion that perhaps the couple had felt threatened, maybe worried, that they wouldn't get their rightful inheritance. Perhaps they'd thought Patience and Felicity would refuse to hand it over.

Now that her cousin had the homestead and all of Uncle John's wealth, Patience had hoped maybe she would be friendlier.

Even if her cousin wasn't willing to make an offer of friendship, that didn't have to stop Patience from making one. She offered a smile. "Good to see you, Cousin. I hope you're enjoying your new home."

Lizette's gaze darted to Gage, as though needing to gain his permission before carrying on a conversation with her.

Gage gave her a slight nod, and she returned the smile, although hesitantly. "We're getting along just fine."

Patience fumbled for something more to say. Should she ask how the chickens were doing? Or the goats? Was Lizette remembering to water the flowers every day? But no, she couldn't ask about those things. What would be the point?

Lizette's attention dropped to Evangeline. "I heard you got married."

"Oh, yes." Patience was grateful the little girl was behaving and remaining by her side at the moment. "This is my daughter, Evangeline Wolcott."

Lizette nodded only briefly at the girl before studying Patience again. "I'm glad you found a place to go."

"That's none of our concern." Gage took hold of Lizette's elbow.

She winced.

Patience couldn't hold on to the same anger that Felicity had toward their cousin. In fact, it appeared that Gage was directing their cousin's actions, that perhaps if she were away from him, she would be friendlier. But Patience didn't trust her own instincts in reading a person's feelings and motivations.

She only had to think of her embarrassing mistake of climbing into bed with Spencer her first night at Trout Creek Ranch to realize how wrong she was at times.

Even so, she could still be hospitable. "I'd love to have you come visit me sometime at my new home."

"Maybe I can—"

"We're busy settling in." Gage's grip on Lizette's arm seemed to pinch tightly. "Now, if you'll excuse us." He gave Lizette no choice but to return her attention toward the counter and Captain Jim, who'd stopped his packaging of the goods to watch the interaction the same as the men playing checkers.

Patience allowed Evangeline to pull her forward, this time toward a display of toys. During the rest of the shopping, Patience caught Lizette watching her from time to time. Was she curious? Full of regret? Or wishing for more of a relationship with her long-lost family than Gage seemed to be permitting?

Finally, with everything she and Evangeline needed to make the surprise for Spencer and the rest of the men busy with haying, they exited the store. Though the skies had been cloudy and rain had seemed imminent at dawn when Spencer left the house, thankfully the clouds had moved on without any rain. Spencer had been worried as he'd sipped a cup of coffee with her in the kitchen before leaving.

After three full days of haying from sunup until well after sundown, Spencer had dark circles under his eyes, but he'd lingered at the table with her again this morning as he had the previous three. Each time, they'd talked more about their pasts and their families. And she'd found that she relished the quiet moments with him and had even begun to wake up earlier in anticipation of the time together.

With the long hours, though, Spencer had been too busy for Evangeline. As a result, the little girl had become more belligerent and difficult to entertain. Just that morning, when Patience had gotten distracted with a project—painting the front steps of the house—Evangeline had wandered off.

Patience had discovered the child in the barn, leading out her pony with every intention of riding out to the hayfield and helping her papa. Thankfully, Patience had found her in time to stop her, although she'd had a difficult time convincing Evangeline not to go. The only thing that had worked was the suggestion to plan a surprise to take out to her papa and the other men.

She guessed the newness of having a mother was beginning to wear off and that the little girl really just wanted to know she was special to her papa.

Patience started down the plank sidewalk with Evangeline skipping along beside her, happy for the moment with her piece of peppermint candy.

A woman in an elegant gown with familiar red hair stepped out of the bank.

Patience's heart squeezed at the sight of her sister. "Felicity!"

The young woman paused and swiveled, holding her hat with gloved hands to keep a gust of wind from wresting it from her head.

Patience picked up her pace. She'd been busy and

preoccupied with her new life, so much so that she hadn't thought much about Felicity and Charity. Now, at the sight of her sister, a swell of homesickness washed through her.

Evangeline somehow kept up with Patience's near run. And as they reached Felicity, Patience threw her arms around her sister and hugged her tight.

Felicity embraced her in return, holding her with a ferocity that told Patience she wasn't the only one feeling the absence.

When they finally pulled back, Evangeline stood between them, looking up at Felicity with curiosity. For several minutes, Felicity spoke with Evangeline animatedly, easily relating to the child, asking her questions, learning her interests, and making her smile.

Felicity would have made a good mother to Evangeline too.

Patience couldn't keep from feeling a sense of relief that Spencer had chosen her and not Felicity. It was selfish of her, but she was glad to have her role as Mrs. Wolcott and didn't want to trade it for anything.

"How is your work for Mrs. Bancroft?" Patience asked.

Felicity's face was paler than usual, and the dark circles under her eyes prominent. In fact, her eyes seemed red-rimmed, as if she'd been crying. "Everything is going just fine."

Patience paused at the ready response. Something didn't seem quite right, but she couldn't decipher exactly what was wrong. Was Felicity unhappy?

"How are you?" Felicity asked before Patience could voice her concern. "I see you've survived your first week of married life. You must be getting along with Mr. Wolcott."

"He's a very fine man."

"Then you like him?" Felicity lowered her voice and darted a look at Evangeline, who was preoccupied with a stray dog passing by.

"I do." She could admit that, couldn't she? So far, in all his interactions with her, Spencer had been nothing but kind and caring.

"Then you don't mind . . . you know . . ." Color flooded into Felicity's cheeks.

Patience didn't know what Felicity was referring to or what was causing the embarrassment. But clearly Felicity was concerned for her well-being and needed to hear her reassurance. "Of course I don't mind. He's tender and patient and considerate."

"Oh my." Felicity raised a hand and fanned at her cheeks. She glanced again at Evangeline as though their conversation needed to be private.

"He's been very busy with haying and tired the last few nights, but I don't mind waking up early to be with him."

Felicity fanned her face faster. "I guess that means I might be an aunt sooner rather than later."

"An aunt? I suppose you are an aunt to Evangeline." Patience tugged at one of the girl's many ribbons.

Felicity opened her mouth to respond but then shifted her gaze to the child.

"Are you my Aunt Felicity?" Evangeline released the mangy mutt and stood, her sticky hands now coated with dog hair.

"I'd love to be your aunt." Felicity managed a smile for the girl.

Another swell of homesickness rose inside Patience, the desire to be with her sisters and to somehow stay connected with them. But she supposed that was what marriage did. It changed the nature of their relationships. "I miss you."

Felicity's eyes turned glossy with sudden tears. "I miss you too."

"You should visit me soon."

At a commotion from inside the bank, Felicity stiffened her shoulders. "Mrs. Bancroft is very demanding and leaves me very little free time."

"Then perhaps I can come visit you soon."

"Maybe." Felicity gave her a quick hug and then started back down the boardwalk at a clipped pace.

In the next instant, a hefty woman poked her head out of the bank. Mrs. Bancroft. Patience hadn't seen the woman often, since she'd been away from Fairplay over the past year on a tour of Europe. But she'd apparently returned sometime over the summer, although no one knew exactly why she'd come back to the remote mountain town.

Her head had a blocklike shape, and her chin and neck seemed to blend together. She wore a wide-brimmed hat with several stuffed songbirds perched around the rim. Her lips were pressed together disagreeably, and the skin beneath her eyes was puffy, only seeming to highlight the frustration brimming in her expression.

"Felicity!" she called. "Stop your dawdling."

Felicity lengthened her stride as she hurried toward her employer.

Patience wanted to call after her sister that she could still come and live with her at Trout Creek Ranch, but she bit back the words, although she wasn't quite sure why. It certainly wasn't because she was worried that Spencer and Evangeline would end up liking Felicity better. Even if her sister was lovely and talented and better at so many more things, Spencer had chosen her. And she couldn't forget that.

13

"You got company, Mr. Wolcott, boss." Tex paused with rake in hand and spat a stream of tobacco between his teeth.

Spencer dragged in a breath of the sweet scent of the hay but didn't stop his raking. Instead, he gauged how much more of the field the hay-raking machine had left. One of the older cowhands was guiding the team that was drawing the long, curved prongs across the field, gathering the cut hay into windrows.

Spencer and the rest of the men were raking up the excess that the machine didn't gather. Some with pitchforks were tedding the windrows they'd raked yesterday, letting the hot sun cure the hay even more.

Maybe by this time next year he'd have an actual tedder machine. He'd never seen one before, but he'd heard the horse-drawn contraption reduced the curing time, since large forks raised and dropped the hay, stirring it up so that the sun could brown it more quickly.

Thankfully he already had a sickle mower, which did the work of ten men with scythes. And thankfully he'd also had the foresight to invest in a horse-drawn hay rake. He glanced again at the contraption behind the team. It wasn't perfect, but like the sickle mower, it diminished the amount of time the haying took.

Even so, they'd been out in the fields for three full days and were now well into their fourth. They had at least two more to go, gathering the hay and transporting it to the barns. His muscles, back, and legs ached—nearly quivered—from the hard work, but every time he peered out over the cut grass, a deep satisfaction filled him.

When he'd come to America, he'd been as broken, spoiled, and weak as a boy. The land had trained him and turned him into a strong and determined man. And now he felt a connection to this place, as if with all the sweat and effort he'd given the land, it had given back to him peace and contentment.

Mostly . . .

"Little Miss and your beautiful bride are heading this way," Tex called again.

His beautiful bride. Spencer's attention swung to her as if she were the sunshine he needed to cure him. Driving the wagon, she held herself with confidence and poise, her long hair plaited, her pretty face as serene as always, her simple clothing molded to her body. Beautiful didn't even begin to describe her. She was breathtaking. Not just now but every time he saw her.

His pulse gave an extra spurt at the remembrance of how she'd greeted him when he'd stumbled into the kitchen this morning. Her hair had been long and loose, not yet plaited for the day. Her eyelids had been heavy with the remnants of sleep. And her cheeks had been rosy, almost glowing.

As she'd clanked around the kitchen searching for a clean mug for his coffee, he hadn't been able to take his eyes off her. The sight of her in her robe and with her hair hanging loose had more than filled him up and been all he'd needed to start his day. He could admit their quiet conversations had become a favorite part of his day too.

When he'd finally forced himself to leave the warm confines of the little kitchen, he'd halted in the door and thanked her. She'd followed him and almost bumped him from behind, so that when he'd turned and steadied her, he'd had the overwhelming urge to caress her cheek, then bend in and steal a kiss.

Many kisses. He'd wanted to bend in and kiss the bare spot at her collarbone and then brush kisses up her neck.

His muscles tightened just thinking about the possibilities.

"Hi, Papa!" Evangeline called from where she bounced up and down on the wagon bench beside

Patience. "We've got a surprise for you!"

The other men had stopped their work now to watch the approach of the wagon. Locusts buzzed all around them, and meadowlarks fluttered about, scolding them for disturbing their nests. The afternoon sun bathed it all in a warm light, including Patience and Evangeline, so that his heart ached just looking at them.

He was forming an attachment to Patience rather hastily. But how could he stop it from growing any more than he could stop the sweet alfalfa from filling his fields?

As she drew the team to a halt, her gaze drifted over the workers as if she were searching for someone. Who?

A moment later, her sights connected with him and stuck there. In fact, she offered him a smile, as if he were the only person in the entire field.

He tossed aside his rake and started toward the wagon, impatient to get his hands on her waist, to feel her, to touch her, even in something as innocent as helping her down.

When he reached the wagon, Evangeline was already hopping to the ground and bounding toward him like one of the bunnies that had made their home under the porch. She was eager to see him, eager to talk to him, more than she had been the rest of the week since Patience had arrived.

She latched on to his hand and gave him no opportunity to assist Patience, and from the corner of his eye, he saw Buck approach her side of the wagon and help her. Even though his foreman only held her hand for a moment during the descent, a knot of protest formed inside Spencer.

As it was, Evangeline dragged him toward the back of the wagon to show him the surprise. And he attempted to focus on her, but even as she tugged off the blanket and revealed the two big pails of cold eggnog that she and Patience had concocted, his body was keenly aware of every move that Patience made as she joined them.

For a short while, all the ranch hands gathered at the wagon, and dippers were passed around. The foamy drink was thick with spices, eggs, and sugar, and was the perfect refreshment for the hot afternoon. There was more than enough for each of the men to have their fill.

Evangeline seemed particularly clingy, wanting to be held every chance that he'd give her. As he stood with the others, she wrapped her arms around his neck and chatted with him nonstop. He realized he'd missed her over the past few days of working so hard and found himself more grateful than before that Patience had made an effort to bring her out to the field, even if just for a short time.

"And so Aunt Felicity said she would be my aunt." Evangeline had regaled him with every last detail of their trip into town, telling him about Patience meeting her cousin in the store, about buying the ingredients they'd needed to make the eggnog, how Patience had indulged her with a piece of candy for being a good girl, and then how they'd talked with Felicity outside the store.

He should have suggested that Patience visit her sister. Surely with how abruptly they'd been cast from their home, she was missing her family.

He let his gaze drift her way only to stiffen at the sight of Buck standing at the back of the wagon smiling up at her. She was kneeling near the pails and smiling shyly at him.

Buck said something else and then laughed lightly, his gaze lingering too long on her.

Was his foreman flirting with Patience?

Spencer thought he'd made it clear that no one was supposed to have anything to do with her. Not even innocently. But Buck had not only assisted Patience down—he was talking with her.

A strange fear gripped Spencer's heart and dug in cold fingers.

"Wait here, darling." Spencer set Evangeline to the ground, patted her head, and then strode toward the wagon bed. He wasn't sure what he was planning to do. All he knew was that he wasn't standing back this time and letting another man claim his wife's affection.

As he reached the back of the wagon, frustration and anger warred within his chest, escalating so that he had half a mind to barrel into Buck like a mad bull and send him flying. His glowering look must have had the same effect as a physical attack, because Buck took several rapid steps backward, holding up his hands as if to ward off an attack.

Rather than take a swing at the man's gut the way his fist itched to, he focused his attention on Patience. His heart was beating wildly like thundering hooves, and his thoughts careened like an out-of-control stagecoach.

She stood, her brows furrowing. "Is something wrong?"

He knew Patience was innocent. That she hadn't meant to smile at Buck. And Buck likely hadn't been purposefully flirting with her.

So what could he tell her? That he was a jealous husband because his first wife had cheated on him while he'd been in America visiting the ranch for the first time? That he'd been devastated to learn about her affair when he returned? That he'd likely never be able to trust another woman again—at least not well?

"Spencer?" Her voice contained a note of worry, and her blue eyes held compassion.

He reached up for her and fitted his hands at her waist.

She released a soft gasp of surprise at his intimate hold.

He could sense Buck's gaze upon him, and suddenly he had the need to show his foreman and every man present that Patience was his.

He lifted her down, and as he did so, he brought her close, letting her body slide against his so that he felt every soft part of her, every exquisite inch. He almost felt as though he were lowering himself into a hot spring and pulling her in with him.

She sucked in a sharp breath, and her questioning eyes met his and seemed to ask him what he was doing.

How could he explain the insanity that was driving him?

With her body still pressed against his, he tightened his grip on her hips. The feel of her tiny waist, the curve of her flesh there, the way his hands nearly spanned her back. He felt it all. Loved how perfectly she fit in his arms and hands.

She opened her mouth, perhaps to ask him again what was wrong. She was so sweet like that. Always concerned about others. But instead of letting her speak, he bent in and took possession of her lips. Not only did he make a claim and slap down every dollar he'd ever earned for it, but he took ownership.

He let himself kiss her with all the longing that had been building from the first day he'd seen her standing in the doorway of her barn. He couldn't hold himself back. Need. Desire. Even jealousy came alongside him and urged him to keep going, to pursue more.

For the first few moments, she didn't respond. Yes, he'd taken her by surprise with the kiss, but her slow reaction was more than that. It was almost as if she didn't know how to kiss, maybe never had kissed a man before.

In fact, he rather liked the notion that this might be her first kiss. And so he slowed down his passion and gently plied at her lips, urging her to join in the construction of this relationship they were building between them.

She responded tentatively, moving and mingling her lips against his. It was enough for him to realize she wasn't pushing him away, was in fact welcoming him in with open arms, maybe even with an open heart.

And why wouldn't she be open to more? He was the one with all of the baggage from his past, not her.

At the moment, all he wanted to do was toss aside the bags and everything else from his previous marriage and just focus on her—taste her, feel her, and learn every nuance about her.

In the next instant, little hands were tugging at his suspenders. "Papa. Mama. Hold me too."

Patience broke away first, her breathing fast, her face flushed, her lips swollen.

He almost groaned with the need to bend back in and kiss her again.

But at the clamp of a hand on his shoulder, the slap of his back, and the laughter around him, he realized the men were now teasing him.

He wasn't ready to let go of Patience, but if he held

her any longer—or kissed her again the way he wanted to—he would never hear the end of it.

Reluctantly, he released her. As he stepped back, he was swallowed up by his men and more of their good-natured bantering.

He managed a grin. "Let's go. Time to return to work."

Although he was tempted to look back at her, he kept himself from doing so. Instead, he made his way toward the windrow. Passing by Evangeline, he bent and placed a kiss on her head. She regarded him with wide eyes, likely unsure what to think of the kiss he'd just given Patience.

That made two of them.

14

Spencer had kissed her.

Patience's knees wobbled, and she grabbed onto the wagon to keep from collapsing. Delicious heat burned low inside her. Her heart pattered as if she'd run all the way from the house to the field. And her lungs were tight and unable to pull in more air.

As he stalked across the field, he held himself with the proud—almost arrogant—bearing of a man who was accustomed to commanding others. He'd just commanded her body and soul. And she'd willingly surrendered to him. Oh, how willingly.

Yes, at first, when he'd settled his hands on her hips, she'd been surprised, even confused. She'd been able to see from the look in his eyes that something wasn't right—although she hadn't known what and still didn't. She hadn't expected him to lift her off the wagon—especially in so intimate a way.

Her body tingled just thinking about the way he'd brought her down, sliding her along his length so that she felt every hard ridge of him against her softness. The sensation had been unlike any she'd ever felt before. It was almost like the move had awakened her. She hadn't known she was asleep, but now her eyes were wide open and every nerve in her body was singing.

How long did she have to go before he held her again?

She was tempted to fan her face with her hand, but she didn't want to draw any more attention her way. Thankfully, the men seemed to be focused on Spencer and teasing him. And the slight grin he gave in return was cocky, as if he'd just won a prize.

Why had he kissed her? Now, after almost a week of marriage?

He'd said he wanted to wait and get to know each other better before sharing the marriage bed. Did he feel that he'd gotten to know her now? Would he want her to come to his bed tonight?

The very thought sent a strange shiver through her. It wasn't one of apprehension. Or dread. Not the way she'd felt the first night of their marriage.

Instead, this was more of a feeling of wanting to be near him, to whisper with him, to have him look at her with tenderness the way he sometimes did. Now, after the kiss, she wouldn't be opposed to him kissing her again. Or pressing their bodies together and feeling all those rigid muscles again.

She flushed and turned to the back of the wagon, covering her cheeks with both hands. What was wrong with her? Why was she thinking such thoughts about him?

She had to stop. Quickly she began to replace the lids on the pots and tuck away the dippers. Even as she did so, she lifted her fingers to her lips. His mouth had been firm, demanding, and passionate. She'd never thought about kissing being so pleasurable. Never imagined what it would be like. Had relegated it to the marital duties to be tolerated.

But she hadn't needed to merely tolerate the kiss. He'd somehow drawn her in so that she'd been an active participant. She'd kissed him in return.

Releasing a soft sigh, she closed her eyes and relived the moment. The swiftness, decisiveness, and hardness of his mouth coming down on hers.

At the memory, need pulsed through her belly—need for him, need for more.

She wanted to kiss him again.

Her eyes flew open and chased after him. He was swiping up his rake from among the cut hay and held himself with as much confidence and determination as before, so that he stood out from the others as the leader.

Was her desire to kiss him again too brazen?

Her thoughts swung to Charity and Hudson and the

way they'd kissed each other. She hadn't understood the connection between them or how they couldn't seem to keep their hands off each other after they were married. But now . . .

Was it natural to begin to feel this attraction to a spouse, for it to grow and develop into a deep passion?

She wasn't sure. But she couldn't deny the growing feelings for Spencer. If only she knew what to do with them.

Over the next few days of finishing the haying, she waited for him to say something about the kiss. Perhaps even secretly, she waited for him to pull her against him again.

But he didn't so much as lay a finger on her.

There were a few moments in passing where she thought she sensed his attraction. One time as he was drinking his coffee in the kitchen with her before leaving for haying, his gaze had lingered on her mouth. Another time, when he'd stumbled into the house after dark covered in sweat and hay, he'd looked at her as though she were a sweet rain shower that he wanted to drink in.

Yet, most of the time he acted as though they hadn't shared the amazing and life-altering kiss in the hayfield. Because it *had* been life-altering. At least for her.

The truth was, she thought about the kiss constantly.

When she was awake. And even more when she tossed and turned in her bed at night in the room next to Evangeline's. During those sleepless moments, she relived the kiss, the starkness of his desire, the passion in his touch.

She hadn't imagined it all, had she?

She almost considered bringing up his suggestion to hire the housekeeper, simply so that she'd have to give up her room and move into his.

But as with every thought she had of Spencer, she pushed it aside, knowing that she had to let him initiate or risk making a fool of herself.

Besides, she had her hands full taking care of Evangeline. Some days were easier than others. In fact, Patience began to see a pattern. When the little girl got to spend time with her father during the evening, the next day went better. But if Spencer was out late and didn't return until Evangeline's bedtime or even after she was asleep, the child seemed to be more anxious and needy the following day.

Patience did her best to distract the girl, and they had numerous projects going. The biggest priority had been painting and decorating Evangeline's room.

However, with the coming of the long winter, Patience knew they would have plenty of cold and snowy days for projects inside. So they spent most of the time outside and completed the renovations on the front of the house. Day by day, the exterior came to life with the colorfully painted rocks, a quilted flag, bright suncatchers, and more.

Of course, Evangeline never stuck to any one project for overly long, which was fine with Patience. She didn't mind taking breaks and finding new and exciting adventures. She used her late evenings, after Evangeline was in bed, to finish things.

Before she knew it, she'd been married for two weeks. With the haying successfully completed, she'd expected Spencer to have more time in the evenings to spend with her and Evangeline. But the very next day, he'd worked with the ranch hands in separating out the steers ready to be driven to the slaughterhouses—some in Denver, a few in the southern part of the state, and others in several of the mining communities. He'd stated more than once that he was ready for the railroad Hudson Vanderwater intended to build in the high country, which would save on the time and resources that cattle drives took up.

When that was finished, he and his men hastened to erect more barbed wire fences along the edges of his property. Though they hadn't had any more of the poisonous larkspur show up on the ranch and kill cattle, they'd had wolves creeping down from the higher elevations and attacking calves.

"Do you think the wolves will come up to our house and try to blow it down?" Evangeline asked as Patience pushed her on the swing Tex had helped her erect in an oak tree next to the house.

The fatherly ranch hand was the friendliest of everyone and stuck close to the barns and corrals. He'd also been at their wedding at the church in town. That had to mean something, didn't it? Was he one of Spencer's closest companions?

"No, the wolves won't come near the house." Patience let the cool evening breeze rush over her face as she peered into the west and the beauty of the setting sun. While the lack of rain had been helpful during the haying, the continuing dry conditions were posing other problems. Spencer had mentioned them just that morning as they'd talked in the kitchen before his leaving, as had become their routine.

Spencer hadn't brought up the word *drought*, but Patience had heard it mentioned when she'd been in town yesterday, purchasing more supplies. Ranchers and farmers were worried about the dry conditions. And Spencer had indicated that the wolves and other wild animals were creeping closer to civilization because they were seeking water and food as their natural sources diminished.

"But in the story, the wolf blows down the houses." Evangeline had begun pumping her legs up and down as Patience had instructed her, but she hadn't gained the power yet to swing by herself.

Patience gave herself a sharp mental shake. Why had she told Evangeline the story of the three little pigs and the big bad wolf? She'd thought the lesson of victory in the end would help alleviate Evangeline's growing concern about the wolves. But it had only increased her worry so that she was bringing up the wolves more.

Patience pulled the swing to a halt and then knelt in front of the little girl, taking one of her hands and looking her in the eyes. She smoothed her fingers over the girl's wrinkled forehead, wishing she could as easily smooth away her anxiety. If only life worked that way. "Have you seen a wolf before, Evangeline?"

She nodded solemnly. "Once, early in the morning. There was one near the chickens."

"Was it as big as you?"

"No. It was smaller."

Patience held out a hand. "Let's go do something."

The child latched on and followed Patience as she led her toward the house. When they were a dozen paces away, Patience halted and motioned toward the house. "Alright, let's see if you can blow down the house."

"Me?" Evangeline's eyes lit up as they usually did at any of Patience's suggestions.

"Yes." Patience guided Evangeline even closer. "Blow hard."

For long minutes, Evangeline ran around attempting to blow down the house. Patience joined her. And finally, laughing, they collapsed into the dry grass in front of the porch.

"We couldn't do it." Evangeline leaned against Patience, breathing hard.

"No, we couldn't." Patience drew the girl into the crook of her arm. "Not even both of us working together."

"Do you think it would blow down if Papa was helping us?"

"Do *you?*"

The little girl shook her head.

"I guess that means if two—even three—of us can't blow down the house, then a little old wolf smaller than you can't do it either."

Evangeline stilled, as though trying to digest the conclusion.

At a distant shout from the field south of the barns, Patience sat straight up, and her body stiffened.

In the fading light of the evening, they could make out several men riding toward the ranch at a frenzied pace. One of them was slumped over, as though injured. The closer they drew, the clearer they became. From the broadness of the back and shoulders of the slumped man, she recognized him at the same time Evangeline did.

"Papa?" Evangeline scrambled up. "Something's wrong with Papa."

Patience's heart began to thud with an erratic dread,

and she pushed up to her feet next to Evangeline. When the little girl began to race toward the riders, Patience stayed right on her heels.

Buck was in the lead, and when he saw her, he called out, "Mr. Wolcott's horse got spooked and threw him."

Spencer was barely hanging on to his mount, his head low, hardly conscious.

"Bring him inside," she shouted over her shoulder as she raced toward the house. "Then send someone to town to fetch the doctor."

She didn't wait to see if they followed her instructions. Instead, she hurried inside and started a pot of water boiling, gathered linen, and turned down the covers.

Only a moment later, the men were clamoring up the steps, carrying Spencer between them. She threw open the door and directed them down the hallway to the bedroom. As they carefully laid him on the bed, Spencer clutched at his shoulder and bit back a groan of pain.

Buck and another man she didn't know hovered around the bed, filling her in on the events and letting her know that Tex was already on his way to town to retrieve the doctor. Spencer was clearly in too much pain to speak and instead cradled his arm and hovered in and out of consciousness.

With Buck's help, she managed to get his shirt off so that she could examine his wounds. He had bruises, but as far as she could tell, he didn't have any lacerations and no broken bones had punctured his skin.

Darkness settled as they waited for the doctor's arrival. With Evangeline's mounting panic, Patience had to leave Spencer's side to attend to the child's needs. She promised Evangeline that she could stay up until the doctor arrived, but only if she changed into her nightgown and got ready for bed.

It seemed hours passed as Patience waited in a chair beside Spencer's bed with Evangeline on her lap. Buck remained at Spencer's bedside on the opposite side, silent and withdrawn.

When the hard pounding of hooves resounded from the direction of town, Buck shoved up and stalked outside. A moment later, he returned with Dr. Steele, the darkly handsome and distinguished man that Astrid had married last year.

During her last trip to town, Patience had heard that Astrid had finally had her baby, a girl, delivered by the town midwife.

Patience rose, hoisting a dozing Evangeline on her hip. "Thank you for coming, Dr. Steele."

"Of course." He offered her a small smile before turning his attention to Spencer. He was a skilled and kind man. If anyone could help Spencer, Dr. Steele was the man.

For several minutes, he examined Spencer quietly and

proficiently. When he straightened, his expression was serious. "He's got a dislocated shoulder."

Patience's heartbeat stuttered. Evangeline, who was awake now, watched the doctor with wide, frightened eyes.

"I'd like you to take your daughter from the house for a few minutes while I pop the joint back into place." Dr. Steele began gently prodding Spencer's shoulder.

Spencer held himself motionless, his eyes closed, his lips pressed together firmly.

Patience nodded. "Will he be okay after that?"

"He's going to be just fine."

With the doctor's confident statement reassuring her, Patience took Evangeline outside and walked with the girl to the stream that ran near the house, letting the flow of the water drown out any cries that Spencer might make while having the painful procedure.

Finally, when Buck stepped outside onto the front porch and gave them a wave, they hurried back to the house.

Buck held open the door with a grin, letting the light spill out. "He's as tough as an old leather saddle."

When they entered the room, Spencer was propped up in the bed with pillows and seemed to be resting more comfortably. His eyes were open, and he took in Evangeline first, then her, likely seeing their distress. "I'll be fine," he said weakly. "No need to worry."

Dr. Steele was packing his bag and paused with a smile. "The biggest challenge now for your wife and daughter is keeping you in bed for the next three days."

Spencer muttered under his breath something about not needing to stay in bed.

The doctor leveled him a serious look. "If you don't rest that joint, you'll risk having your shoulder slip back out of place much more easily in the future. You need to give it time to heal."

Spencer closed his eyes, but not before Patience saw the frustration darkening the green-brown. She didn't know how she'd be able to manage both him and Evangeline at the same time. But she was determined to try.

15

Three days in bed was torture.

Spencer sighed and tossed his book onto the bed beside him. His shoulder was still sore, but it was far better than it had been the night he'd dislocated it.

The kitchen door squealed open, and the patter of feet running through the house told him Evangeline and Patience were back.

Thank the Lord in heaven above.

Evangeline's shorter and quicker steps drew nearer, and a second later she came bounding into the bedroom. She stopped short and called over her shoulder. "He's back in bed, Mama."

"Of course I'm in bed." He smiled and held out his arms to her.

With a beautiful smile in return, she dashed over to him. She was about to throw herself upon him but halted and carefully slipped her arms around him in a hug.

Neatly dressed with her fair hair in braids, she smelled of sunshine and wind.

"*Of course?*" Patience appeared in the doorway a moment later and cocked her head toward the window. "You do know that we could see you walking around."

"And I was walking briefly because my arm is sore, not my feet." Even though he'd tried to follow the doctor's orders, he couldn't endure much more lying around.

Not that he'd minded the extra time with Evangeline and Patience. He'd actually loved every minute of their sweet devotion and attention. And he'd loved watching and listening to them interact.

Although he'd known Patience was a good mother from what he'd witnessed before being bedridden, his admiration of her mothering skills had grown. She was constantly busy, drawing Evangeline into every activity and giving the little girl so much to do.

They'd decorated his room with colorful objects, created a card game to play with him, made him gifts, served him various sweet concoctions, acted out a story with costumes, and a dozen other activities.

He realized that Patience flitted from one thing to the next like a delicate songbird flying to different branches, always full of life and energy. She loved taking the time to admire the little things, often got sidetracked, but always thoroughly enjoyed every moment.

And it was clear she was teaching Evangeline to do the same.

If he'd thought he was attracted to her before, he liked her more than ever after spending hours with her while he was an invalid. He liked her genuineness, her straightforwardness, and even her naivety. She was simple and kind and truly caring.

Was it possible he was even starting to fall in love with her?

The prospect scared him. But he'd known going into the marriage that he couldn't ignore his attraction to his wife forever, that eventually he'd have to move beyond the marriage of convenience. He just hadn't expected his feelings to develop so quickly.

With how utterly alluring she was, he supposed it had been inevitable. She was simply irresistible. Especially when she was looking at him the way she was at that moment, with her eyelids halfway lowered, her face flushed, and her lips slightly parted.

The memory of the kiss they'd shared that day haying was never far from his mind. He'd told himself after kissing her that he'd made a mistake, that he'd done it in a fit of jealousy, that it hadn't meant anything. He'd refrained from being in proximity to her and had stayed busy enough that exhaustion had kept him from a repeat.

But now? Today? He wasn't busy. He wasn't tired. And he had no reason *not* to kiss her. Or at the very least he wanted to touch her.

Would she let him?

He knew exactly how to find out . . .

He sat up and swung his legs over the side of the bed.

As soon as he did, she shook her head and started toward him. "You know the doctor's orders."

He waited quietly.

She neared him, pressing her lips together in determination, lips that were usually rounded so softly but were now firm with her resolve.

All he could think about was cupping her jaw and having those lips against his with just as much determination. Her mouth moving against his. His mouth joining hers. The rhythm and tempo increasing.

Zeus.

As she stopped in front of him, he let her gently push against his chest in an attempt to force him back onto the bed. Instead of obediently falling back, he did the unthinkable. He slipped his arms around her waist at the same moment that she shoved him harder. The momentum propelled him backward, and he took her with him.

She gasped and tumbled on top of him, careful to avoid his injured shoulder.

Glorious heaven. Her body pressed against his so that he was suddenly aware of every single inch of her soft curves melding into him.

Her startled face hovered just inches above him. Such graceful lines of her jaw, high cheekbones, pretty arched brows, and those long lashes. Her blue eyes were filled with innocence and sweetness. She had no idea how to play games or to entice or lead a man on. In fact, he could almost see the remorse beginning to form in her mind, an apology starting to shape her lips.

Before she could issue her regret, he wrapped his uninjured arm around her thoroughly, giving her no reason to doubt he'd orchestrated the move on purpose and had intentionally drawn her down on top of him.

But was she ready for him to do something so familiar? He had the feeling she wouldn't protest, would allow him to pursue his own pleasure with no consideration for herself. That was likely the view she had on marriage and love.

He wanted to change that. Could he show her that she would find enjoyment with him every bit as much as he intended to find it with her?

His fingers caressed up her spine, memorizing each slight indenture. And he started to lift his head, intending to kiss her again and kiss her thoroughly.

Her breath caught, sending her chest pressing against his. Then she slid a glance away from him toward Evangeline standing at the end of the bed, watching them curiously.

He let his head drop back to the mattress.

At the clearing of a throat at the bedroom door, he looked past Patience to find Tex stepping into the room, waggling his eyebrows. "Want me to take Little Miss out to the barn? I've been meaning to show her how to saddle her pony."

Spencer had half a mind to take Tex up on his offer.

Patience didn't wait for his answer and was already pushing against him to free herself. All the wiggling only made him more aware of her body and his desire for her. But he had the decency of mind—barely—to release her.

If only he'd had the chance to kiss her first. Even just a small kiss.

But he suspected he wouldn't have been satisfied with something tiny. That he would never be content with stolen kisses once in a while.

Patience was already scurrying from the room, fanning her cheeks.

Tex sauntered toward the bed, grinning as if he'd been the one to orchestrate the entire encounter. As he lowered himself into the chair, he waited until Evangeline followed after Patience before he spoke in a half whisper. "Reckon you'd have an easier time smooching with your wife if you had that housekeeper to keep an eye on Little Miss once in a while."

Tex had been making some progress in that regard, had two inquiries to the notice he'd posted, but he hadn't done anything more about it since the accident.

"Very well. Do your best to hire someone soon."

"Will do, Mr. Wolcott, boss."

Spencer scooted back against his pillows, ignoring the satisfied grin that stretched over Tex's leathery face. Even so, he couldn't ignore the need that was growing inside him, the need to put aside his fears and allow himself to have a real marriage. His heart warred within him to use caution, to not give away his heart so easily again.

But with a woman like Patience, he was learning, it was all too easy to throw caution aside and give her his heart totally and completely.

16

Sitting at the desk in her room, Patience pressed her hands to her cheeks again. Even hours after Spencer had pulled her down on top of him on the bed, her face flamed every time she thought about the incident.

What had it all meant? And why had he done it?

He hadn't touched her again the rest of the day, not even by accident. But every once in a while, when she'd been in his bedroom, she'd felt him studying her with intense interest. Maybe it had even been desire. She wasn't sure, and for the hundredth time today, she wished she were better at reading people's emotions.

She stared at the mosaic tiles in front of her, the newest project that she'd started for a sundial to go near the flower gardens outside the front door. The simple ceramic tiles of various colors sat scattered over the desk. Untouched tonight. Unable to hold her interest.

Nothing had held her interest after the encounter

with Spencer. He'd filled every nook and cranny of her thoughts so that she'd been more scattered than usual, spilling, forgetting, and fumbling her way through just about every task.

She'd almost been relieved when Evangeline's bedtime had arrived and she could tuck the little girl away in her bed where she'd be completely safe. Patience simply didn't trust herself when she was this distracted. She could hardly keep track of herself, much less another tiny human being.

Absently she picked up a tile, her mind going back to the first night of her marriage when she'd sat in this very chair and thought about Spencer and whether she should go down to his bed.

Was that what he wanted again? Had toppling her onto the bed been his way of signaling that he wanted her to join him at night from now on?

She could admit she'd been breathless with the desire to feel his lips upon hers again. Would he have kissed her if Tex hadn't shown up?

She skimmed her lips as if that could somehow capture the moment again so that this time it ended in his mouth pressed against hers.

Delicious warmth spread through her.

She stood.

Yes, he wanted her. She had to go down to him.

Quickly she sat.

What if she went to him and was wrong? What if he sent her away?

Her mother's warning from over the years pushed to the forefront of her mind—that she wouldn't be good enough for a husband.

Although Spencer hadn't seemed to mind her imperfections, he was from a wealthy family who would expect him to have a graceful and poised wife, someone with charm and manners.

She was far from any of that.

Even if her flaws didn't deter him now, eventually he would see them and get tired of her, wouldn't he? A part of her couldn't help but wonder if that was why he'd suggested hiring a housekeeper—because he wanted the house tidier and more orderly and was already exasperated with the messes she left in her wake.

At a soft tapping against the front door downstairs, she rose again. As she exited her room, she cast a glance toward Evangeline's bed, now surrounded by the enchanted forestland. The little girl was asleep, having been entirely manageable the past few days with Spencer at home. She'd almost been like a new person with her papa there spending hours with her.

The rapping sounded again, this time louder. She hurried down the stairs, wanting to get to the door before it woke Spencer. Even as she reached the bottom and started through the hallway, Spencer was already ahead of her and nearing the door.

Words of scolding were at the tip of her tongue. She needed to tell him to get back in bed, that she would answer the door. But with the late hour of night, she guessed he'd never listen to her, wouldn't want her anywhere near the door without knowing who was there and why.

"Who is it?" he asked, his hand on the lock.

"It's me. Buck."

The foreman, like Tex, had been in several times over the past few days to check on Spencer, bringing news and updates on everything having to do with the ranch and the cattle.

Even though the hallway was dark, lantern light spilled out of Spencer's open doorway, illuminating enough that she could see he was shirtless. The bruises surrounding his shoulder were discolored, but every sharp line and angle of his body was cut in hard stone and never failed to draw her attention and make her want to pause and simply admire him.

But he was already opening the door, throwing it wide to reveal Buck, holding a rifle, his expression grim. "Sorry for disturbing you, Mr. Wolcott." Buck tipped the brim of his hat toward Patience where she'd halted just outside the bedroom door. "Ma'am."

Spencer glanced her way too. If he was surprised to see her in the hallway, he didn't give anything away—at least, that she could see.

"What is it?" Spencer turned back to Buck.

"The fellas on guard duty caught a couple of ranch hands from Stirrup Ranch in the act of cutting the fence."

"Do they still have them in custody?"

"Yep. And more of the Stirrup ranch hands showed up, and things ain't lookin' pretty, if you catch my meaning."

Spencer held his foreman's gaze, a silent message passing between them, likely one they didn't want her reading.

"Figured you'd want to know." Buck shifted his rifle. "Came back to get more of our fellas and weapons."

Spencer shook his head. "I don't want this turning into a war, Buck."

"Then what do you want me to do?"

A long pause filled the night, so that the lone howl of a wolf rose eerily in the distance.

Spencer rubbed at the back of his neck, a move he seemed to resort to whenever he was frustrated. Then he released an exasperated huff. "Saddle my horse. I'm going out with you."

"No." The word slipped from Patience before she could hold it in.

Buck shot a glance her way, but Spencer didn't acknowledge her objection. "Round up as many men as you can. I'll do what I can to negotiate. But we also have to be prepared to fight."

To fight?

Before she could say more, Spencer had closed the door on Buck and was striding back down the hallway.

"You can't go." She was tempted to grab him as he passed by. Instead, she kept her hands by her sides and followed him into the bedroom.

"I have to." He crossed to his chest of drawers.

"The doctor said that when your three days abed are finished, you still need to restrict your activity for a few more weeks."

"I've rested far longer than necessary." He yanked open the top drawer and pulled out an undershirt.

He began to tug it on. She wished she were bold enough to watch his every move, but she turned away to give him his privacy.

As he finished, she waited quietly, trying to find the right words that would convince him to remain behind, to let his men handle the conflict. But after getting to know him, she suspected no amount of pleading would change his mind. He wasn't the type of man who would sit back and let others face danger while he waited in safety and comfort.

As he brushed past her and exited, he hesitated, but then he continued toward the front door.

She followed and stopped just outside the bedroom.

His footsteps echoed down the hallway with resolve,

and her heart quivered with strange dread at the danger he would face, not only by going out too soon after his accident but in the possible shoot-out with neighboring ranch hands.

She couldn't keep from reaching out a hand toward him. "Spencer?"

Only a few feet from the door, he halted, his back facing her.

What did she want to tell him? She wasn't sure, so she said the first thing that came to mind. "Please be careful."

He nodded but otherwise didn't move.

She drew in a shaky breath.

The sound seemed to draw him back around. He glanced at her outstretched hand, then lifted his eyes to her face. She wasn't sure what he read there—perhaps invitation. Whatever it was, he started toward her with long, hard steps.

The dim light in the hallway kept his face shadowed, but there was no hiding the determination in his gaze.

Her stomach quivered. Determination for what?

She didn't have to wait long to discover it. As he reached her, he lifted his hands to her face, cupped her cheeks, then angled in and captured her lips decisively and powerfully. The momentum pushed her back against the wall. His body pressed against hers, flattening her and possessing her all in the same movement. His mouth moved against hers hard, as though he were a dying man partaking of his final feast. And his body encompassed her—all of him, his solidness, his scent, his power. He left her with no choice but to respond, to arch into him and taste of him in return.

She was thoroughly overwhelmed. It was as if the kiss were taking her and Spencer to the highest mountaintop, where the sun was hot and wove around them so that their hearts and breaths were one.

But with a final thrust, he brought them back down. In the next instant, he tore his mouth from hers and strode to the door. He tossed it open, stepped out, and let it close behind him without a look back.

She could only stand motionless against the wall where he'd left her, her body tingling, her mouth aching, her heart thudding erratically as sweet, desperate longing pulsed through her.

What did all this desire mean?

Was she falling in love with Spencer?

Her fingers splayed against the wall in an effort to keep herself from sliding into a heap on the ground. What else could such intense attraction be if not love?

She closed her eyes, the longing for him swelling again.

Did he feel the same way? Was he finally giving himself permission to care again for another woman?

She just prayed she would be everything he needed and that for once in her life she wouldn't fall short.

Patience stretched in bed, not wanting to awaken from the dream of kissing Spencer. This time, they were on his bed after he'd pulled her down on top of him, and she allowed him to touch his lips to hers. The light kiss quickly turned hard and consuming, making her stomach coil with need.

"Oh my." She opened her eyes and hugged her arms to her chest. The dreams were only making her hungrier for Spencer—hungrier for his presence, his touch, his intensity, his kisses, and yes, even his pressing her against the wall.

Bright sunlight broke through the haze of her desire.

For several seconds, she admired the way the light slanted through the dangling pieces of colorful glass in the window—crimson, royal blue, gold, emerald.

Sunlight?

What time was it?

She took in the dangling glass and then the bright canopy of leaves overhead. She was in Evangeline's bed, and the angle of the light told her it was well into the afternoon.

Patience shot up, her hand flying to the spot next to her.

It was empty.

"Evangeline?" She scrambled off the bed, her skirt tangling in her legs. Her eyes and body still felt heavy from exhaustion. But she had to wake up from her unintended nap and find Evangeline before the child got herself into trouble.

Picking up her skirt, she rushed into the hallway and toward the stairs.

How had she allowed herself to fall asleep? She'd only meant to rest beside Evangeline as she did from time to time, but she hadn't slept well the past two nights that the men had been involved in the conflict out in the west pasture.

She'd only gotten brief bits of news when Tex or one of the other men had come riding back for more ammunition. Apparently, they were in a standoff with the Stirrup Ranch men and fighting over a long stretch of fencing. The Stirrup Ranch cowhands had stripped away the barbed wire. And whenever the Trout Creek men attempted to string it back up, the neighboring cowhands shot at them.

No one had gotten injured. Yet. But the situation was precarious.

Apparently Spencer had attempted to negotiate, had even ridden over to Stirrup Ranch to talk out the problems. But he'd been met with bullets there and had been forced to turn back.

"Evangeline?" She hurried down the stairway. Earlier, when Evangeline had started yawning and had grown especially belligerent, Patience had coaxed her into bed for a short respite with the promise of creating something special that they could send out to her papa.

The girl had been agreeable, had closed her eyes, had even fallen asleep. Or at least, she'd pretended to.

Once in the downstairs hallway, Patience poked her head first into the kitchen and then into Spencer's bedroom. With each step she took, her body tightened with growing frustration at herself. She shouldn't have fallen asleep, much less gotten carried away with reliving Spencer's kisses.

As Patience reached the front rooms of the house, she already knew Evangeline wasn't there. And her heart began to pick up pace at the sickening possibility of where Evangeline might have gone.

She burst outside onto the front porch and glanced frantically around the yard. The sun was closing in on the west, which meant the afternoon was almost over. Now that autumn was nearing, the evenings were growing darker and chillier sooner.

Without bothering to hunt anyplace else, she went directly to the horse barn. With all of the ranch hands that could be spared out on the west fence line, the ranch yard and the barn were deserted.

As she headed down the long center aisle between the rows of horse stalls, her heart pattered out a rhythm of dread, yet she held out a sliver of hope that her worst nightmare wasn't coming true.

At the end, she glanced into the stall that was home for Evangeline's pony.

It was empty.

"No!" The cry burst from Patience. For an agonizing moment she simply stood frozen, her mind conjuring the image of the precious little girl riding her pony into the middle of a gun battle, the bullets whizzing around her.

Bile rose swiftly into Patience's throat, and she had the urge to bend over and be sick. But she didn't have time for that. She had to leave and go after Evangeline. She didn't know how long the child had been gone, and perhaps there was still time for her to catch up and keep Evangeline away from the danger.

Numbly, Patience rushed to the stall for the horse that she'd used on another occasion or two. She didn't want to take the time to saddle the creature, but she also didn't know if she could ride bareback without falling off. With shaking fingers, she eventually managed to cinch the saddle, but not without several cries of frustration.

Without bothering to go back into the house for her bonnet, she rode hard and fast toward the west edge of the property. All the while, she scanned the open fields and rolling hills for any sign of Evangeline upon her pony. But the landscape was barren and deserted. Not even a steer to be seen, only the gophers poking their heads up from their mounds and chattering at her for disrupting their peace.

She kicked her horse faster, her heart pounding in tempo to the beating hooves.

Why hadn't she done a better job with Evangeline?

A sob rose up in her throat. She knew that Evangeline became harder to manage every time Spencer got busier. She should have realized earlier, before the nap, that Evangeline was misbehaving because she was anxious to be with her papa. Patience should have found a better way to reassure the little girl that she'd see her papa again soon.

Ahead, Patience caught sight of a slip of blue. Her pulse lurched. Evangeline had been wearing a blue dress today with blue ribbons in her hair.

"Evangeline?" she shouted, slashing at her reins and digging in her heels, needing the horse to somehow magically start flying.

As Patience crested a low hill, she glimpsed the blue again . . . and blond hair.

Patience couldn't hold back the sob. It was Evangeline. "Evangeline! Stop!"

At the same moment she caught sight of the child, she also saw a dozen or so men ahead, lying on their stomachs with guns positioned over logs and rocks. A short distance beyond them, through a torn and broken fence, more gun barrels glistened in the late afternoon sunshine. And the guns were pointed toward Evangeline . . .

"Hello, Papa!"

At the familiar voice, Spencer's head snapped up, high enough that the Stirrup Ranch fellows could have put a bullet right through his hat if they'd wanted.

He dropped back down and then glanced behind him. At the sight that met him, his blood froze. "Devil it."

Evangeline was riding directly toward him, bareback on her pony, her braids bouncing on her shoulders, her pretty—and clean—face wreathed with a smile that was for him alone.

What was Evangeline doing out here? Now? And where was Patience?

At a desperate cry not far behind Evangeline, he saw Patience upon her horse, riding wildly, frantically, calling out for Evangeline to stop.

He knew at once what had happened—the same thing that had happened dozens of times over the past months since Evangeline had learned to ride the pony. She'd found a way to get out from her caretaker's watchful eye and had come out to the field to visit him.

Except this time, her impertinence was much too dangerous. Quite possibly even life-threatening.

Sweat rolled down Spencer's spine, sticking his shirt to his back. Dust and grime coated every inch of his skin, including the skin not showing. Grit even lined his mouth and nostrils. Not only was he dirty, but he was also exhausted. And to make matters worse, his injured shoulder was aching more with every passing hour.

If Evangeline got any closer, she'd be in range of the Stirrup Ranch fellows. And the same with Patience. The men could start shooting. At his daughter and wife. And harm them.

Curses upon him. He refused to let his daughter and wife come to any harm over this fence line. In fact, he'd rather get shot at himself than let anyone take aim at them.

"Evangeline! Please!" Patience called out again, her voice breathless. She was drawing too near.

Protest swelled within him. He had to stop them both. "Stay back!" he yelled, waving an arm at them.

Evangeline slowed but kept coming. "I've missed you, Papa!"

"It's too dangerous out here, Evangeline! Return to your mama at once."

The smile faded from her face and her lips wobbled. "I want you, Papa! Not Mama."

Tex had rolled across the ground and was now beside him, his expression frantic. "We've got to keep them back, Mr. Wolcott, boss."

Over Spencer's shoulder, from the direction of the Stirrup Ranch fellows, came the sound of a gunshot, the crack echoing in the dry air.

Spencer's heart leapt into his throat. And he did the only thing available to him. He jumped to his feet, held up his arms, and shouted at the Stirrup ranch hands. "You win! We'll tear the fence down."

The gun barrels swiveled away from Evangeline and Patience and trained on him instead. That was better. As long as he could keep the attention on himself and off his family, he'd die a happy man.

Evangeline had finally halted, her eyes widening at the sight of all the guns. A moment later, Patience reached the child, reined in her horse, and slid down.

He had to distract the ranch hands. "No more fighting!" He raised his voice higher. "And no more shooting."

She was at Evangeline's side in a heartbeat, pulling the girl down into her arms and running toward a large boulder that was only a dozen feet from their horses. A second later, she crouched behind it with Evangeline, shielding the little girl with her entire body.

Even though they were safe, his pulse was still beating erratically, like a dozen cannons booming through his bones.

He was done with the fighting. What good would it do to battle over this piece of fencing, for his right to erect the barbed wire, for his need to protect his land and his cattle . . . only to lose what was most important to him—his wife and his child? The two people he loved more than life itself. He may as well admit the truth— that he loved Patience in spite of all the warnings he'd given himself to be careful.

He stood in the sun, the dust swirling around him, the silence broken by the desperate, whispered prayers of Tex, who was lying nearby, still under cover.

Spencer swept his gaze over the property that he'd worked so hard to manage, the land that he'd driven himself to control. Dry, rocky, covered in shrubs. It wasn't even all that pretty.

What did it matter how much more land he gained, how many more cattle he owned, and how big his ranch became? What was the purpose in all of that if he didn't have anyone to share it with?

"You made your point," he called again to the Stirrup Ranch men. "And for now, I'll stop putting up the barbed wire on this side of my property. But your foreman has to agree to meet with me to discuss the matter and work out our differences civilly."

He waited silently, this time gazing directly at the gun barrels.

A moment later, several of the guns disappeared. A weathered old fellow began to stand, slowly, cautiously. Spencer recognized him as the foreman.

He gave the foreman a nod. "Let's call a truce and go home."

The fellow narrowed his eyes upon Spencer. "How do we know we can trust you?"

Spencer's thoughts raced in an almost frantic effort to come up with a solution. He could only land on one. "I'll have my men finish tearing this line of fence down today. Hopefully that will prove to you I'm a man of my word."

The foreman stared at Spencer for several more seconds, then he grunted. "Fine. Reckon if you do that today, I'll be ready to chaw tomorrow."

Spencer motioned at several of his men and then at the fence.

Tex was standing beside him now. "I'll stay out here with the men and get this done. You're needed elsewhere." He glanced toward the boulder where Patience was still hiding with Evangeline.

A lump of emotion pushed into Spencer's throat. He gave Tex a silent look of thanks, then started toward his wife and daughter. As soon as he reached them, he knelt beside Patience and placed a hand on her back.

She startled and lifted her head away from Evangeline's. Tears streaked her face.

Evangeline was softly sobbing too. And at the sight of him, she wiggled to free herself from Patience.

He lifted her into his embrace, and she wrapped her little arms tightly around his neck, squeezing him.

A whoosh of air left his lungs, and he sagged where he knelt, the reality of all that had happened crashing into him. He hugged Evangeline harder. Something had to change in his life. He wasn't exactly sure what, except that he needed to make sure he didn't lose the people who were most important to him. He'd do anything to keep them. Anything at all.

18

Patience couldn't face Spencer. She stood in the hallway just inside the front doorway, the shadows of night hiding her.

The rhythmic creak of the porch swing told her he was still there. Watching for her. Wanting to talk about all that had happened. Waiting for an explanation for why she'd put his daughter into life-threatening danger.

He hadn't said so. But all evening as he'd spent time with Evangeline—pushed her on the swing, sat with her on the porch, and cuddled with her in her bed—he hadn't once brought up the obvious question: Why had Evangeline been unsupervised long enough that she could ride out into the midst of a gun standoff?

Surely he wanted to know.

Patience drew in a shuddering breath. She hadn't been able to stop the inward shudder since the moment she'd seen Evangeline riding in the direct line of fire of the guns. And she hadn't been able to stop the tears. She swiped a hand over her cheek and brushed away the wetness.

How could she explain herself? She had no excuses. She'd neglected Evangeline. Plain and simple.

Her mother's warnings clamored in her head louder than ever. The day when she'd been sixteen and her father had granted permission for Abner Turner to court her, she'd been so excited and had spent the day getting ready for his visit. Instead of making things beautiful, she'd made a mess of everything.

She'd accidentally let the chickens loose when she'd gone to gather eggs for a custard she wanted to make. Only after she'd put the custard in the oven had she noticed the chickens running loose. She'd run outside to gather the chickens back into the coop. But while dashing after them, she'd gotten distracted with picking a bouquet of flowers only to be drawn back to the house by the smoke pouring from the kitchen windows.

When she'd rushed into the kitchen, the wall near the stove had been on fire. Thankfully, Felicity and Charity had been close at hand and had helped her put out the flames before they'd spread to the rest of the house.

Her mother had returned from shopping to find the chickens still loose, wilted flowers strewn over the doorstep, crusty dishes and baking supplies unattended, the stench of burnt custard wafting through the smoke, and the blackened kitchen wall smoldering.

As Mother had stood with her hands on her hips and surveyed the disaster, she'd leveled a severe glare upon Patience. "You may as well cancel Abner Turner's visit. He'll never want you for a wife. No man will."

No man would want her for a wife.

Patience dropped her head against the wall as more tears squeezed out and ran down her cheeks.

She'd hoped her mother was wrong, that maybe Spencer would want her. He hadn't seemed to mind her scattered and messy habits. In fact, after the kiss a couple of nights ago, she'd almost allowed herself to hope he was beginning to truly like her.

But now . . .

The squeaking of the swing came to a halt.

Was he coming inside to look for her?

She squared her shoulders and braced herself for the confrontation. She couldn't avoid it forever.

"How is everyone?" Outside, the soft question with the faint Mexican accent belonged to Tex. His bootsteps plunked on the steps leading up to the porch.

"Safe." Spencer's voice was soft in reply. Was that relief in his tone?

She pictured the way he'd stood when she'd ridden up to Evangeline. The terror etched into his face as he'd realized the precariousness of the situation. His eyes had held a desperation she'd never be able to wipe from her memory. It had matched her own.

All she'd been able to think about was getting Evangeline away from danger. She hadn't cared about anything else. And clearly Spencer hadn't either.

The truth was that her recklessness and irresponsibility could have killed both Evangeline and Spencer. And the realization stirred cold fear deep inside. Things may have turned out this time, but what would happen the next time she failed?

"You get the fence down?" Spencer asked.

"Yep. Rolled up the devil's rope and had it carried back to the barn."

Not only had she brought danger to Evangeline and Spencer, but she'd caused Spencer to lose his battle with the neighbors. She knew how important the fence was to him in keeping out wolves and other predators as well as containing his cattle.

She bit back another shudder.

"Can you hire a housekeeper tomorrow?" Spencer's question was loaded with tension.

"I can try."

"See that you do."

"Even if one of them agrees to the position, I can't guarantee they'll be able to come out right away."

"Offer them a bonus to get here as soon as possible."

Patience closed her eyes. Spencer didn't want her to be alone with Evangeline any longer and wanted a housekeeper to oversee them. He didn't think she was capable of taking care of his daughter any longer.

Why had she ever thought she'd make a good mother and wife?

Maybe he should have married Felicity instead of her. Felicity would have been the better candidate. And he'd seemed interested in Felicity, hadn't he?

Patience pressed a hand against the ache in her chest. What had Evangeline said that first day when she'd arrived at the ranch? It had been something like *"Papa said you'd have red hair."*

Why had Spencer told Evangeline her new mother would have red hair?

A strange new tremor began to wind through Patience. Was it because Spencer had expected to marry Felicity at the church that morning instead of her?

Her mind spun back over the events that had unfolded, starting with Spencer coming out to the homestead that evening and questioning her. He'd asked if Felicity was home, had wanted to know Felicity's age, had asked if marriage would be more agreeable to Felicity than being a nursemaid. He hadn't asked any of those questions about her.

Then at the church the next morning, he'd asked where Felicity was, hadn't wanted to begin the ceremony without her there, and had even brought it to a halt when Father Zieber had started without Felicity.

Had Spencer looked confused at that point?

Patience had been so nervous she hadn't been paying attention to him. Even if she had been aware of his reactions, would she have understood what his emotions meant?

Why had Tex taken Spencer outside the church? Had it been because he'd needed to persuade him to go through with marrying the wrong sister?

He'd refused to kiss her after the wedding ceremony. Was that because he hadn't been attracted to her? If Felicity had been standing before him, would he have kissed her? Felicity with her pretty red hair. Felicity who was smart and organized. Felicity who would have paid attention to Evangeline and known how to train her better.

Tex said something else to Spencer, but the clamor in Patience's mind was too loud to hear anything else. In fact, the roiling in her stomach pushed upward into her throat so that she felt as though she was going to be sick.

She pressed a hand against her mouth and quietly began to back up.

What had she done?

The truth was growing clearer with each passing moment. She'd made a huge mistake. She'd thrown herself at Spencer and had all but forced him to marry her when he'd wanted someone different. That was why he'd sent her away on their wedding night, wasn't it? Because he'd thought he was getting the vivacious and beautiful Felicity. Instead, he'd ended up with her.

Of course, after they were married, he'd clearly been trying to make the best of things with the wrong sister. He'd probably allowed himself some attraction, if the kisses were any indication.

But that didn't erase the horrible truth of the matter. Spencer Wolcott hadn't intended to marry her in the first place.

She reached the stairs and could hardly race up them fast enough. She tried to keep her tread soundless—didn't want to draw Spencer's attention tonight, not when she was so humiliated.

When she made it to her room, she closed the door and crept to her bed. She didn't bother changing into her nightgown. Instead, she pulled the covers up to her chin, buried her face in the pillow, and let the silent sobs loose.

She wasn't sure if it was minutes or hours later when she heard footsteps coming up the stairs. She recognized the firm and determined tread. Why was Spencer coming upstairs? To check on Evangeline again?

She buried a sigh into her pillow. Maybe she needed to go to town and confess to Felicity what had happened and see if her sister would be willing to take her place as Spencer's wife. Felicity clearly hadn't been happy working with Mrs. Bancroft. Maybe marriage to Spencer would be more preferable, especially if she knew that Spencer had wanted her. Then Patience could seek out Father Zieber, explain the mistake to him, and ask for an annulment.

The very thought of separating from Spencer sent a stab through her heart, one so painful she could hardly breathe. She wasn't sure she could give him up. How could she relinquish him and watch him with another woman, especially her sister?

But if it would make Spencer happy, then she had to do it.

His footsteps started down the hallway.

Besides, Felicity would make a better mother to Evangeline. Even if the prospect of leaving Evangeline was as painful—or nearly so—as giving up Spencer, Patience had to make herself do what was best for the little girl.

And staying wasn't best for Evangeline. Today's death-defying encounter was proof of that.

Patience quieted her thoughts and racing heart as the footsteps drew closer. When they slowed outside her door and then stopped, she held her breath. She'd expected him to continue toward Evangeline's room. What was he doing at her door?

At a soft tap, she nearly jumped but somehow managed to hold herself motionless.

He paused, as if waiting for her response. Finally he whispered, "Patience?"

Of course he still wanted to discuss what had

happened earlier. And he deserved answers. It was only right that she humble herself and confess she'd fallen asleep, that she hadn't been paying good enough attention to Evangeline.

But she couldn't talk to him tonight. Not when she was mortified by the magnitude of her mistake in convincing him to marry her instead of Felicity.

As the doorknob turned, she rapidly faced the wall and closed her eyes. Why was he coming into her room?

She made herself breathe evenly and forced herself to stay calm even though everything inside her was on edge. She couldn't possibly look into his eyes and perhaps see there what she'd missed all along, that he'd never wanted her. Just as her mother had predicted.

The door creaked open. Not very far. Likely enough that he could view her in bed.

He was silent a moment. Then the door closed with a soft click. His footsteps continued toward Evangeline's room. Patience could hear him inside stepping around her bed, could picture him tucking the blankets up over Evangeline more securely, just as he'd done earlier. Then his footsteps returned down the hallway but this time passed by her room without halting.

A part of her wanted to sit up and call to him and admit she really was awake. She wanted to throw herself at him, tell him she was sorry, and beg him not to cast her away but to give her another chance.

But another part bit back the words. She'd already humiliated herself enough, hadn't she? She had to keep a sliver of her pride intact.

As his footsteps faded down the stairway, a deep sob worked its way up, and hot tears stung in her eyes. She buried her face into her pillow so that Spencer wouldn't be able to hear her crying.

If only she hadn't made such a mess of things. But it was the one thing she excelled in—making messes.

Except this time, she intended to right all the wrongs and make things better. It was the least she could do for the little girl and the man she'd grown to love.

Patience leaned back against the wagon bed and hugged Evangeline in the crook of her arm. The dirt road leading away from Fairplay was worn and smooth and only jostled them a little. But Patience wanted every excuse she could get to hold Evangeline.

"I'm sorry, Mama," Evangeline said again as she had already a dozen times over the morning.

Patience leaned down and kissed the top of the girl's head. "You don't need to worry."

But Evangeline peered up, her big blue eyes filled with worry—a worry that hadn't gone away no matter how much Patience had tried to reassure her.

Evangeline was clearly sensing something was wrong, but Patience couldn't say anything about her mission to find a replacement for herself as wife and mother. Not yet.

"You alright back there?" Tex asked from the wagon

bench where he sat beside Buck.

"We're just fine." Patience smiled again at Evangeline.

The little girl smiled back, but her dainty face was still wreathed with concern. And she slipped her hand into Patience's, as though to connect herself even more.

A wagon rolled down the road toward them, and Tex slowed the team and swerved to the side of the path to make room.

The September sun overhead had lost some of the heat of the summer, but it was still warm and bright. Too bright on Patience's tired eyes.

After a restless night, she'd awoken with the unchanged conviction that she had to convince Felicity to be Spencer's wife and Evangeline's mother instead of her. She'd sought out Tex and asked if she and Evangeline could ride into town with him. He was going to interview the potential housekeepers, and Buck had gone along to give an update to the sheriff regarding the barbed wire war.

Unfortunately, when Patience had called upon Felicity at Mrs. Bancroft's house, the butler had told her that Felicity was unavailable. No amount of pleading had changed his mind.

She'd loitered near the house for a short while, hoping Felicity would somehow be able to sneak outside and meet with her. But as the hour had passed without sight of her sister, she'd walked with Evangeline down Main

Street, hoping she'd encounter Felicity exiting one of the establishments like she had previously.

Unfortunately, Felicity hadn't been anywhere in sight, so the trip had been unsuccessful. She'd finally resorted to leaving a short note for her sister regarding the need to step in as wife and mother since that's what Spencer had wanted.

Meanwhile, she'd decided that until Felicity could take her place, she would enjoy every last second of the time that she had together with Evangeline.

As the wagon from the opposite direction rumbled past, Patience sat up straighter at the sight of their old gelding Stan pulling the wagon. Impeccably attired in a suit, Gage stared straight ahead, his lips pressed in a firm line beneath his dark mustache. In another gaudy gown that showed an abundance of cleavage, Lizette cast a glance over her shoulder at Patience. Was she trying to communicate something?

Patience wished again, as she always had, that she were better at reading people's expressions and emotions.

If she'd been better, maybe she wouldn't have made such an embarrassing mistake with Spencer that day when he'd come out to the homestead. As it was, she'd been mortified to be around him earlier in the morning. She hadn't been able to look at him and had made sure to occupy herself entirely with Evangeline all the while he'd lingered at the house before he'd headed out to the barns.

She knew she couldn't avoid the difficult conversation with him forever, not only about what had happened yesterday with Evangeline but also about the marriage mix-up. But for now, she hadn't gathered the courage to speak to him about either one.

She lifted a hand in greeting to Lizette and tried to offer a smile as well. Lizette nodded and then glanced at Buck.

Buck had shifted on the wagon bench and was watching Lizette. Patience didn't have to wonder about the meaning of his stare. His interest in Lizette was obvious. Was the low-cut neckline revealing too much of her bosom and enticing him? Or perhaps he was enamored with the prettiness of her features.

Whatever it was, Buck shouldn't be ogling the woman.

"My cousin is married, Buck." Patience spoke quietly so that her voice wouldn't carry and embarrass Lizette.

Buck's gaze homed in on Lizette even more, although she'd turned to face forward now, and not much more than her profile was visible. "That's your cousin?"

"Yes, her name is Lizette. And her husband's name is Gage."

"Lizette and Gage?" Buck watched the retreating wagon. "What's their last name?"

What was her cousin's married name? Patience couldn't remember it. "I don't think she informed me."

"That's odd." Buck's eyes narrowed on the couple. He didn't say anything else, but he remained unusually quiet for the rest of the ride home.

Evangeline was more subdued too. And as Tex pulled the wagon to a stop in front of the house, Patience helped the girl down, settling her on the ground only to have little arms circle her neck and refuse to let go.

"I promise I won't be naughty again." Evangeline's eyes brimmed with tears.

Patience hefted the child to her hip and walked with her to the front steps, now painted a pretty shade of blue and lined with the painted rock animals that she and Evangeline had made. She sat down on the bottom step and pulled Evangeline onto her lap.

"Listen to me." Patience brushed a hand over the child's cheek. "We all make mistakes. None of us are perfect." She ought to know. "The important thing is to learn and grow from our mistakes so that the next time, maybe we can do just a little bit better."

"I'll do a lot better the next time. I promise." Evangeline brushed a hand over Patience's cheek.

Patience wanted to smile at the way the little girl imitated her. But the smile fell away as she peered down into the blue eyes and saw herself there. Making the same promise to her mother as a little girl. Wanting to please, wanting to make her happy, wanting to earn her love.

Tightness formed at the back of Patience's throat.

Even with all her efforts, she'd never measured up. In fact, she couldn't recall ever earning her mother's love. If she had, her mother had never spoken of it. Not even on her deathbed.

She didn't want Evangeline to feel the same way, as if she had to earn love and affection and approval. "Darling." The pet name Spencer used for Evangeline rolled off Patience's tongue naturally. "I want you to know something."

"What?"

"I want you to know that I love you. I love you when you're good. And I love you when you're naughty. I love you when you're happy. And I love you when you're sad. I love you when you do a lot. And I love you when you do a little. I love you when you're neat. And I love you when you're messy."

"Do you love me when I'm riding my pony out to see Papa? And love me when I'm here with you?"

Tears sprang into Patience's eyes. "Yes. I love you then too."

Evangeline laid her head against Patience's shoulder and sighed. Was it a relieved breath? Was it really that simple to alleviate the child's worries? To reassure her of how much she was loved no matter what she did or didn't do?

Yes, she supposed it was that simple. If her mother had reassured her the same way, maybe she would have learned to love herself. Instead, she only saw all the faults, the same faults that her mother had always pointed out.

Perhaps it was time to accept herself, faults and all. And learn to love herself anyway. After all, she couldn't expect Evangeline to do what she herself wasn't willing to try.

Across the yard, Buck had descended from the wagon and was striding back toward her. "I figured it out," he called to her. Was his voice laced with excitement? If so, why?

Patience wasn't ready to release Evangeline just yet. As with the wagon ride, she wanted to enjoy every moment with the child, because all too soon, her time at Trout Creek Ranch would be coming to a close.

Buck didn't stop until he towered above her. With his grin in place and his hat tilted at a rakish angle, he might even be considered handsome by other women. But compared to Spencer, he looked like a boy and not a man.

The truth was, no other man could even begin to compare with Spencer. Not in maturity, handsomeness, and character. He was in a class of his own.

"I figured it out," Buck said again.

"I'm not sure what you mean." Patience, as usual, felt two steps behind.

"Your cousin."

"Lizette?"

"Her real name is Lucy."

"No, her name is Lizette. It's written in my uncle's Bible."

"Lucky Lucy."

"But—"

"She's from Gold Bar Saloon up near Leadville."

Patience was trying to read Buck's face but couldn't understand the direction of the conversation. "My cousin was living in a saloon in Leadville?"

"She's not really your cousin."

Setting Evangeline down, Patience stood, a strange unease prodding her upward. "Have you met my cousin to know this for certain?"

"Lucky Lucy is a—" Buck slid a glance toward Evangeline. "Let's just say I spent some time with Lucky Lucy when I lived up in Leadville."

Patience stared at Buck. He was trying to tell her something, but was he holding back because Evangeline was present? "You courted her?"

Buck snorted, but then stopped short as he took in Patience's expression, likely seeing the confusion there.

She glimpsed Spencer in one of the corrals among his ranch hands and the steers. "Evangeline, why don't you go say hello to your papa."

Evangeline hesitated.

As if Spencer had sensed their attention upon him, he paused what he was doing to look their way.

Evangeline smiled and bounded toward him. "Hello, Papa!"

Buck waited until the little girl was out of hearing range before speaking again. "Lucy's a woman of ill repute."

Patience took a step back at the vulgar declaration. "But she's married to Gage."

"Don't know a hound's hair about Gage. But he's got a shifty look about him."

She couldn't argue with Buck about that. Gage had been so negative that even she'd picked up on the fact that something wasn't quite right about him.

"If I had to hazard a guess," Buck continued, "I'd say Gage cooked up a plan with Lucy to come down and pretend to be a long-lost daughter so they could get their grubby hands on all the gold."

"But they have my uncle's Bible and letters he exchanged with his wife."

"John's first mine was up near Leadville, right?"

"Yes, that's where he lived after he moved to Colorado from California."

"Then it's possible he might have left some of his things behind. Or maybe lost them. And if a good con man stumbled across them, it wouldn't be too hard to come up with a scheme to pretend to be John Courtney's relatives."

All of Buck's assumptions were beginning to make

sense. "What about Lucy's red hair?"

"My guess is that's why Gage chose her to be his partner, because he reckoned the red hair would cinch up the lie real tight."

"Goodness gracious." Patience wavered.

Buck steadied her, but then in the same instant he darted a glance toward the corrals and released her quickly. "If Mr. Wolcott's look could kill, I'd be a dead man right about now."

Evangeline had reached the corral fence, climbed up, and now stood with her arms looped around the top post. She chatted away with Spencer, who had crossed to her but was staring at Buck.

Buck tipped the brim of his hat and started to back away from Patience.

Turmoil rolled through Patience. She wasn't ready for the conversation with Buck to come to an end, wanted to know what she ought to do. Should she talk with Felicity? But after this morning's failed attempt, maybe she needed to start investigating first.

"I'll go visit Gage and Lizette—Lucy."

Buck halted, almost tripped. He shot a glance toward Spencer and then lowered his voice. "That ain't a good idea."

"Why?"

"For a lot of reasons."

"I won't say anything about our suspicions. I'll just

see if I can learn more about them."

Buck rubbed a hand down the scruff on his cheeks and chin. "Fine. I'll go with you tomorrow night. But you can't say anything about this to anyone. If Gage and Lucy know we're on to them, they'll clean out the bank and leave town faster than a wet whistle."

"Maybe I can come up with an excuse for the visit?"

"Reckon that's a good idea." Buck gave a curt nod and then began to stride toward the corral, steering far clear of Spencer, who was watching him with narrowed eyes.

Patience sat back down on the porch step, her heart heavy under the weight of all that Buck had revealed. If Lizette really was Lucy and an imposter, then she had to do what she could to bring that to light. But how could she possibly do so without making matters worse than they already were?

Spencer's chest was tight and his muscles tense. They had been for the past couple of days since Evangeline and Patience had ridden out into the middle of the gun battle and his entire life had come to a glaring halt.

"Higher, Papa!" Evangeline called from the swing.

As she came hurtling toward him, he prepared to give her a more forceful push. But at the sight of Buck and Patience on their horses, leaving from the rear exit of the barn, his heart crashed to the bottom of his chest.

In the next instant, Evangeline and the swing thudded against him. The unexpected force sent him toppling backward, off-balance. Before he could catch himself, he landed on his backside on the hard packed earth. The impact jarred his shoulder, sending pain shooting up and down his arm.

What was Patience doing with Buck? And why were they sneaking out a back way as though they didn't want to be seen leaving together?

Buck glanced from side to side and then quickly led the way north. Patience followed closely behind him. From her stiff shoulders and the way she'd pulled her straw hat low, he could tell she was uncomfortable and didn't want anyone to notice her leaving.

Spencer tried to drag in a breath, but his airways seized.

He'd thought yesterday that he was only imagining the interest between Patience and Buck as they talked by the house. But if watching the two talking hadn't already been difficult enough, the moment Buck had touched Patience, Spencer had come undone. He'd been tempted to stalk over and shove Buck, but the foreman had quickly moved on, no doubt sensing the disapproval.

Spencer had burned with anger and resentment for hours afterward, and he hadn't been able to speak with Buck, had been worried he'd punch him. So he'd stayed well away from his foreman the rest of the day. And later, when he'd gone inside for supper, his suspicions and anger only added to the growing silence between himself and Patience.

Patience had already been unusually quiet since the gunfight incident. Although he'd wanted to talk to her about all that had happened, wanted to make sure she was okay, wanted to apologize for Evangeline's behavior, the moment had never been quite right to discuss it.

Of course, Evangeline had filled the gap with her chatter and liveliness. And Patience had been as kind and loving to the little girl as always. But something had set Spencer on edge. He hadn't been able to pinpoint exactly what was wrong. He'd considered the possibility that he was being irrationally jealous. That he still had trust issues with women after what had happened with Honora.

But now . . .

His heart ached as painfully as his backside at the possibility that Patience could so easily cast him aside for another man. Even if she wasn't hitching up with Buck, she was pushing him aside. He could feel it as tangibly as if she'd shut a door in his face.

"What's wrong, Papa?" Evangeline was using her feet to drag herself to a stop, peering at him over her shoulder, her blue eyes wide with concern.

What could he say to her? That he'd fallen hopelessly in love with Patience? And that now he was an irrationally jealous husband?

Because the fact was, deep inside, his gut told him that Patience was too sweet to ever go behind his back and have an affair with a man like Buck. After the past few weeks of being married to her, he'd gotten to know her well enough to see that she didn't have a hurtful bone in her body. She'd never be unfaithful to him. And she'd never willfully do anything that would cause him any grief.

"Papa?" Evangeline hopped from the swing before it came to a full halt. She landed like a nimble barn cat and then raced toward him. "Did you get hurt?"

He was hurt. Even all this time after Honora's betrayal, the wound hadn't gone away.

As Evangeline reached him, she held out a hand as if she intended to help him to his feet. "You'll be okay, Papa. It's just a little bump."

It wasn't just a little bump. And he wasn't sure that he'd be okay. If an incident like this with Patience and Buck could tear him up this much, how would he ever be able to have a normal relationship where he wasn't constantly seeking out trouble?

He shouldn't have married Patience. He should have followed his instincts, shouldn't have given in to the pressure to find a mother for Evangeline. In some ways, he'd unconsciously believed that giving Evangeline a mother would fulfill the little girl. But the gunfight had shown him that even when she had a mother, she still needed him to increase his efforts and be the father she needed.

He pretended to allow Evangeline to pull him to his feet. Once he was standing, he couldn't keep from staring down the wagon path. Even though Buck and Patience were no longer in sight, their retreating backs were seared into his mind. He didn't want to think about them. But the jealousy ate at him until he could no longer stand himself.

Finally, with Evangeline in tow, he headed to the bunkhouse that Tex shared with half a dozen other ranch hands. He was disappointed that Tex's housekeeper interviews from yesterday hadn't elicited any results.

But he should have known finding a housekeeper wouldn't be easy. After all, he'd never had an easy time hiring a nursemaid. Maybe he'd have to place an ad in an Eastern newspaper.

Evangeline had admitted that Patience had been sleeping beside her when she'd decided to get up and visit him in the west field. If he'd provided Patience with a housekeeper or been more involved with Evangeline for himself, maybe she wouldn't have been so tired.

Holding Evangeline's delicate hand in his, he knocked against the door of the bunkhouse. The logs were gray with age, but the chinking between them was new and fresh in preparation for the upcoming winter. The few windows were open, and laughter and the good-natured teasing of the fellows spilled out into the cooler evening air.

Tex swung open the door, shoving on his hat and shrugging into his coat in the same motion. "I take it you're going after them, Mr. Wolcott, boss?"

Spencer should have guessed that Tex would know about Buck and Patience riding off together. A steer couldn't have a bellyache in the farthest field without Tex knowing about it.

"Where did they go?" Spencer didn't care that his tone was clipped and demanding.

Tex stepped outside and closed the door behind him. His brown, leathery face contained a worry that set Spencer on edge. "Buck said he was taking Patience over to visit her cousin."

Why tonight? And for what purpose? He waited for Tex to elaborate, but Tex gave a shrug that said he didn't know more.

Spencer certainly couldn't find fault with Buck for accompanying Patience. In fact, Spencer wouldn't want Patience riding the distance by herself, not so late in the evening. Anything could happen, and he would rest easier if he knew she was with an experienced cowhand.

If only Tex had taken her instead of Buck.

Tex hooked the bottom button of his coat and then smiled at Evangeline. "Reckon I can give Little Miss that lesson on saddling her pony."

What if the visiting of the cousin was an excuse for the two to go off alone? The image of Buck pulling Patience into his arms flashed into Spencer's mind. His gut clenched hard in protest.

She was his wife and his alone to kiss. And yes, he wanted to kiss her again more than anything. But he'd restrained himself, using up a year's worth of self-control to stay away from her after that kiss in the dark hallway earlier in the week. Zeus. He hadn't been able to stop himself from striding back to her and taking a kiss. The power of it had nearly made him forget his mission. His body still heated just thinking about how he'd pressed her hard against the wall and allowed himself a moment of feeling every luscious part of her body connecting with his.

If Buck so much as thought about it . . .

Spencer swiped off his hat and ran his fingers through his hair. He was being paranoid again. He couldn't race after Patience every time she decided to go someplace or anytime she was with another man.

"I'll be fine." He took a step back, drawing Evangeline with him. "I'm sure they'll be back soon enough."

Tex paused in his buttoning.

Spencer hadn't told anyone about the humiliating end to his marriage with Honora. But sometimes he wondered if Tex had been able to read his mind and learn of it. Or if perhaps the rumors had reached this far side of the world.

Tex stared at him a moment, then nodded. "If you need me to give Little Miss a lesson, I'll be in the barn."

Spencer began to lead Evangeline away, forcing himself to walk calmly, even though everything within him wanted to run frantically after Patience.

He had to learn to trust her. And he had to start today.

21

As the homestead came into view, Patience's stomach cinched with nervousness.

She and Buck had discussed possible strategies on the short ride over. Buck had suggested telling Lucy and Gage that she'd forgotten something as a reason for the visit. And since Patience had forgotten several paintbrushes in a drawer in the sideboard, she'd decided to inquire after them.

Once they were actually inside the house, Buck wanted Patience to ask Lucy for information about her uncle and father's family that any daughter ought to know. In doing so, Buck hoped to confirm his suspicions.

"You don't think she'll recognize you?" Patience plodded beside him down the narrow lane that led to the house and barn.

"She might." Buck was eyeing the surrounding area warily, his hand resting on his pistol at his hip. "But I reckon I was just one face among many she's seen over the years."

The very implication sent mortification through Patience's body, all the way from her ears to her toes.

"But who knows? Maybe she'll recognize my handsome face right away, spill it all, and blow her cover."

If only it would be that easy. Patience was praying it would be so.

They passed by the bristlecones that lined the wagon path. Standing tall with their twisted and gnarled branches, they were like lone old men keeping watch over the homestead. The weeds along the wagon path had grown tall, but the grass and shrubs were yellowed and dry. And the pots of flowers she'd carefully watered and tended all summer were wilted and dead.

The chickens pecking about their fenced-in coop seemed fine, although there were fewer in number. Had Lucy and Gage cooked and eaten some? Or had the wild creatures sneaked in to take their fill?

She didn't see all the goats wandering about grazing. But that didn't mean they weren't somewhere, perhaps in the barn. How was Stan faring? Had the old gelding received enough tenderness?

As she and Buck reached the front of the house, a curtain pushed aside in one of the front windows, but there wasn't any other movement. She dismounted and started up the front steps, taking in each of her creations with fondness, but also thinking of all the artwork now gracing the home at Trout Creek Ranch.

Somehow the new ones were even more special because they'd been crafted with her daughter. Even if Evangeline wouldn't be her daughter for much longer, Patience would cherish the many memories they had together and would never forget about the girl, even when she had a new and better mother.

Stifling a sigh, Patience knocked on the door, then stood back and waited, her mind flooding with the memories of the past year of living in the charming home with her sisters, their boarders, and then most recently Hudson.

Yesterday when she'd gone to town on her attempt to visit Felicity, she'd stopped by the telegraph office to see if they'd received word yet from Charity. But as with every other time she'd inquired, there was nothing from their sister. After over a month on their honeymoon, surely Charity and Hudson would be returning to Baltimore and get the frantic messages she and Felicity had sent. It wouldn't be long now before Charity responded.

Maybe after this evening she'd have enough evidence to prove that Lucy and Gage weren't really who they claimed to be. Then she'd be able to contact Charity and tell her everything was resolved.

After a lengthy silence with only the nearby call of a

hawk, likely fishing in Juniper Creek, Patience rapped against the door again.

A moment later, it opened a crack, and Gage peered at them from the other side. His brow was furrowed above irritated eyes.

"Good evening." Patience tried to keep her voice friendly. She probably should have told Buck that she was terrible at pretending anything and was a terrible liar.

"What do you want?" Gage didn't budge with the door and eyed Buck, who stood behind her.

Maybe Buck should have stayed on his horse and let her do this alone. Did it look too suspicious to have him there while she retrieved paintbrushes?

"I was hoping I could visit with my cousin and get to know her a little better." The words rushed out before she could stop them. She couldn't force herself to continue using the name Lizette if the woman's name really was Lucy. She hadn't been sure if she would be able to say the word *cousin* either. But thankfully she'd done at least that.

"She's busy." Gage started to close the door.

Buck pushed forward and wedged his foot into the space before Gage could shut the door. "And Patience needs to get a few paintbrushes she left at the house."

"She can go buy her own paintbrushes now." Gage's voice dropped a notch. "She's married to a rich gentleman."

Through the crack in the door, Patience caught a

glimpse of Lucy. She was standing in the middle of the sitting room, wearing one of her lowcut gowns, her red hair pulled up into a knot. Perhaps the gown was one she'd worn while entertaining men at the tavern. The very prospect mortified Patience, and she dropped her gaze to Buck's boot stuck in the door.

A part of Patience wanted to back away, to leave, to avoid the confrontation. She never had been very good at facing conflict. She normally let Charity and Felicity handle those kinds of issues and offered them her encouragement and support.

But at the moment, the duty of saving the homestead from an imposter fell upon her shoulders. If she ran away, she might lose out on the chance to uncover the misdeeds of this couple and expose them for being frauds.

She had to remain strong.

"Please, Gage." Patience tried for her kindest and gentlest voice. "You can't control who my cousin can or can't see forever."

Gage's lips lifted on one side in the beginning of a smirk. "Oh, I can control your cousin for as long as I need to."

Patience could sense that this man was indeed sharp and quick-thinking. Probably too sharp and quick-thinking for a simple mind like hers. How could she win against him when he'd likely thought of all the angles for solidifying his and Lucy's story?

Patience released a sigh.

Buck must have taken the sigh as the sign that she was giving up, because he shoved his leg through the door and then his whole body. Since he was a big and muscular man, Gage had no chance against him and had to fall back.

"I'll have you arrested for trespassing," Gage shouted.

"Go right ahead and try." Buck stepped farther inside.

Tentatively, Patience followed, taking in the disarray—unwashed dishes scattered across the table, empty liquor bottles lining the windowsill, gaming cards strewn about. The floor was coated in dust and dirt, the air was rank with cigar smoke and stale food, and the living area was disorganized with discarded clothing and shoes and blankets.

Patience had never been inside a tavern, but she suspected this was what one might look and smell like.

Lucy was watching her with rounded eyes. Were they filled with guilt? Maybe the guilt had been there in Lucy's expression all along because she knew she was lying and deceiving. And maybe she hadn't wanted to be a part of the scam.

Patience smiled at the young woman. Whatever Lucy's role was in the whole charade, surely a little kindness would put her at ease. And maybe honesty was the best way forward after all. "I'm sorry that you're in this situation."

"What situation?" Lucy's gaze darted to Gage.

As with the last time Patience had witnessed the interaction between the two, she had no trouble seeing that Gage was directing what Lucy could say and do.

"I'm sorry that Gage is using you for this scheme." The words tumbled out.

From near the door, Buck's muttered curse told her she'd said the wrong thing.

"Gage isn't using me." Lucy stuck out one of her hips and rested a hand against it.

Before Patience could figure out how to respond, a hard metal barrel dug into her back. The pressure was so sharp and painful that she cried out.

"Don't move"—Gage's voice came from behind her—"or I'll shoot her."

Gage aimed the statement toward Buck, who had his hand on his pistol at his belt but hadn't withdrawn it.

"Whoa, now." Buck held up his hands. "No need to get so riled up. We came for the paintbrushes. That's all."

"Is that what you're here for, Patience?" Gage rammed the gun against her spine.

She couldn't keep from crying out again.

"Tell me the truth." Gage pivoted, drawing her in front of him so that she was acting as a shield, so that if Buck did manage to fire off a shot, he'd risk hurting her.

"Lucy, please." She turned her attention upon Lucy, hoping the young woman had a shred of compassion inside. "If you do the right thing, I'm sure we can reward you with a sufficient amount so that you no longer have to work in the tavern."

Lucy, of course, glanced at Gage before responding. "My name's not Lucy, and I don't work in a tavern."

"That's not what Buck said."

"Buck"—Gage jabbed the barrel into her again—"doesn't know what he's talking about."

Buck was shaking his head at her. He was signaling something, but she couldn't figure out what.

She guessed she needed to stay quiet, probably should have stayed quiet all along.

"Put your weapons down," Gage demanded to Buck, "or dear cousin Patience is going to get hurt."

Slowly Buck placed his revolver on the dining room table.

"Your knife too." Gage's voice remained hard.

Buck slipped a knife out of his belt and set it on the table too.

"Now, out the door."

Buck hesitated.

Before Patience could say or do anything, the handle of the gun slammed down against her shoulder. She cried out, the pain of the impact so sharp she wavered, blackness hovering in her vision.

With Gage half dragging her, she managed to stumble outside and around the house. And Buck seemed to be cooperating more quickly, likely to keep Gage from hurting her again.

As they reached the trapdoor mounted on stones that led to the cellar, Gage issued instructions for Lucy to unlock the chain and lift the hatch, revealing the dug-out hole that provided storage for food during the winter. No larger than eight feet by eight feet, it was crowded with empty baskets and crates awaiting the harvest of the root vegetables. The dirt ceiling was low, so that Patience had always needed to crouch whenever she went inside.

Gage made Buck climb down first. Then he steered Patience toward the edge and shoved his boot into her back so that she toppled down.

Thankfully, Buck caught her. As his arms wrapped around her, the door above them slammed shut and darkness settled heavily. At the clink of the chain slipping back into the handle, Buck set her aside and launched himself against the door.

For several long moments, he rammed it hard, trying to open it. But though the plank lifted an inch or two off the stone perimeter, the chains were already in place and locked. And no amount of muscle power would be able to break them loose.

As though recognizing the same, Buck finally ceased his efforts and released a slew of curse words under his breath.

No doubt he was angry with her and wishing they

hadn't come. He didn't have to say anything for her to know she'd made a mess of things.

Not only had she ruined their chances of finding a way to convict Gage and Lucy of their crimes, but now she and Buck were trapped with no one knowing where they were or what had happened. But at least they were alive. They could be thankful Gage hadn't shot them when he'd dumped them in the cellar, especially since they knew such incriminating information.

At the clatter of the door above, the slab lifted an inch or two, enough to reveal several wiggling and slithering creatures being shoved through with a pitchfork.

A distinct rattling echoed in the damp air. And her blood turned cold.

That type of rattle could only mean one thing. Rattlesnakes.

In the next instant, the creatures fell to the floor next to them, and she screamed.

Gage did intend to kill them after all, except he was doing it in a way that would keep anyone from blaming him.

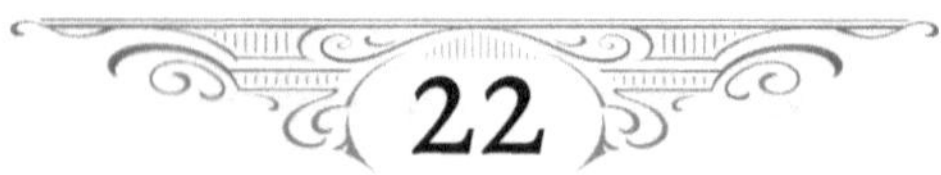

22

Darkness had fallen, and Buck and Patience still hadn't returned to the ranch.

Spencer paced the front porch, his footsteps tapping out his frustration and worry. Tex waited on the swing, pushing back and forth with the tip of his boot. Evangeline sat beside Tex, curled up at his side. Even though Spencer had tried to put her to bed, she hadn't been able to settle down without Patience.

If Patience really had gone to visit her cousin, she surely would have been back by now. Why wasn't she?

His gut churned. Had the visit to the cousin merely been an excuse for the two to have a secret rendezvous?

No, it couldn't be. Patience wasn't like that.

Even with all the effort to force his mind from the image of Patience within Buck's embrace, he couldn't shove it away. Somehow her face was getting mixed with Honora's so that the memory of walking into his home and into his bedroom was filled with pictures of Patience and Buck instead of Honora and her lover.

No. He stopped short, rubbed at the tension in the back of his neck, and then shook himself free of the images.

Even if Patience wasn't like Honora, she shouldn't have gone off with Buck alone. Didn't she realize that no one was safe from temptation? That everyone needed to be careful? That a small friendship could lead to more?

"You may as well ride out and see if they're alright," Tex finally said.

"Do you think Mama is hurt?" Evangeline's question was faint and frightened.

"Buck is with her and won't let anything happen." At least, Spencer hoped so.

"What if they got attacked by wolves?" Evangeline asked.

"Buck's got a gun. And he's a good shot."

Even as Spencer tried to alleviate Evangeline's worries, he knew Tex was right. He wouldn't rest until he rode out and checked on Patience.

With a kiss to Evangeline's head, he took his leave. The ride over to the Courtney homestead didn't take long. As he trotted down the lane, the darkened windows of the two-story home told him no one was there. The moonlight revealed a shabbiness and unkemptness to the place, different than what it had been like when he'd ridden out a few weeks ago. Clearly the new owners weren't taking care of the homestead as well as the Courtney sisters had.

Halfway down the lane, he reined in his horse. He was obviously wasting his time in searching for Patience and Buck here. He may as well return home and keep waiting.

Or what if they'd landed in danger? There were still outlaws who made Colorado their home. It was possible they'd been accosted.

He shook his head. Everything he'd told Evangeline was true. Buck was too sharp, would know what to do to protect them.

The only other option was that Buck and Patience had gone to town. But why? Had Patience wanted to see her sister? That had to be the reason.

With a fresh burst of determination, Spencer aimed his horse toward Fairplay. Less than ten minutes later, he was riding down Main Street. Many of the establishments were busy in the evening, light falling from windows onto the dusty street, men coming and going, laughter and music wafting out of open saloon doors, the roasted scent of beef lingering in the air.

He passed by the businesses and turned onto one of the side streets that led to the wealthier and bigger residences, including the Bancroft home, where Patience had indicated Felicity was working. He'd met Mrs.

Bancroft once or twice and hadn't particularly liked the woman. As a noblewoman, she'd snubbed him because his family wasn't of the peerage but was instead landed gentry.

His father hadn't had titles and wealth handed to him, had instead worked hard to invest and make a name for himself. The investment in the ranch had been a huge gamble. But it had done well. And even though Mrs. Bancroft considered him inferior, Spencer held his head high, knowing he'd worked hard like his father and could be proud of all he'd accomplished.

He dismounted in front of the elegant home in the popular Victorian style, three stories with cylindrical turrets, gabled roofs, and too much ornamentation for his taste. The light coming from the windows illuminated the pink color of the house along with dainty white trim.

He secured his horse, then ascended the stairs to the front door. He knocked as decisively as always. Then he waited.

When a manservant opened the door a moment later, Spencer pulled himself up to his full imposing height. "Mr. Wolcott for Miss Felicity Courtney."

The servant darted a glance over his shoulder to the hallway. As if the elaborate green wallpaper with gold etching wasn't ostentatious enough, the dozen busts of Roman gods lining each side of the entryway made it more garish. "Miss Courtney is unavailable."

Spencer guessed that the servant had strict orders to limit the visitors that came calling on Felicity. Nevertheless, Spencer didn't consider himself an ordinary caller. In fact, he wasn't afraid to use his wealth and connections when he needed to.

"I expect you to announce my presence to Miss Courtney straightaway." His voice turned clipped. "I must see her."

The manservant paused as though he was considering arguing with Spencer. Then he bowed his head and scurried down the hallway and disappeared into one of the rooms, likely the dining room.

Spencer waited only a moment before his impatience prodded him. He stalked down the hallway until he was standing in the open doorway of the dining room. A half a dozen people sat at an elaborately set table with a bouquet of roses in the center and candelabras glowing on either side. They were wearing their finest evening attire, and the scene reminded him of home, of his mother's dining room and the beautiful dinners and parties she always had—except that the portly Mrs. Bancroft sat at the head and regarded him with raised brows.

In a stunning blue gown, her red hair arranged fashionably, Felicity rose, her wide eyes upon him questioning and worried.

As she moved from her spot and began to approach him, Mrs. Bancroft spoke. "If you do not sit back down at once, then you can pack your bags and leave tonight. You shall no longer be welcome here."

Felicity halted, her thin shoulders stiffening. Her jaw clamped together, the muscles twitching as if she were holding back from speaking her mind with only the utmost restraint. "I believe Mr. Wolcott is here regarding my sister. And I would like to speak with him."

"Your sister is Mr. Wolcott's responsibility now, not yours." Mrs. Bancroft motioned at Felicity's chair, her rings and bracelets glittering with opulence. "Now sit."

"I shall only be a moment, ma'am." Even though her eyes flashed with obvious frustration, her tone was calm.

Mrs. Bancroft pushed away from the table and stood, laying her linen napkin beside her plate too meticulously. "Very well, Miss Courtney. If you choose to cast aside my training and instructions, then I refuse to have you under my tutelage any longer."

Was the old woman threatening to fire Felicity from her job simply for meeting with him? He didn't want to be the cause of her demise. And yet, Mrs. Bancroft was clearly being unreasonable.

"Would you like me to come back another time?" Spencer asked Felicity in a low voice.

She hesitated a moment longer, then braced her shoulders and lifted her chin. "No. As a matter of fact, Mrs. Bancroft, you don't need to have me under your tutelage. I resign from my position."

Mrs. Bancroft drew in a sharp breath, but the young woman marched from the dining room.

When she stopped in the hallway, she shuddered and then released a short laugh, almost as though she couldn't believe she'd had the pluck to quit her job.

Mrs. Bancroft was still calling to her, demanding that she return to her spot at the table. But Felicity strode to the end of the hallway and stepped out onto the front porch. He followed.

In the darkness, she peered up at him. "Mr. Wolcott, I take it you've come to see me about Patience realizing the mix-up in marrying you."

"Mix-up?"

"She said you'd intended to propose to me."

Spencer's stomach bottomed out. "Devil it." He should have explained everything from the start and been honest with Patience. Except that if he had been, then he might not have married her. She surely would have been mortified at the misunderstanding on her part and would have gone to Felicity and attempted to convince her sister instead.

And the simple truth was that he was relieved he'd married Patience and not Felicity. Yes, he'd been hesitant to marry someone who looked like his late wife. But Patience was so different than Honora that the similarities in appearance hadn't ended up mattering. He'd been worried for nothing.

"She wrote me a note when she came to town a day or so ago. She explained the mix-up and insisted that I become your new wife and Evangeline's new mother."

Spencer shook his head. "No offense, Miss Courtney. But I'm not interested in having anyone but Patience."

Felicity's lips curved up into a pretty smile. "Good. Because I'm not interested in trying to replace her."

"Because of my own cowardice in facing my past, I initially believed that I wanted to ask you, but Patience is the right woman for me."

"Then you need to reassure her that she's doing a fine job."

"She is."

"She doesn't think so. She believes she's failing at it and that you and your daughter need someone better."

"She's just what we need—"

"Then you have to tell her that too. Because she feels the need to step aside."

Spencer silently cursed himself. Did this have to do with what had happened with Evangeline the other day? Evangeline was impulsive at times. Her riding out to the field to find him had occurred other times before Patience had moved to the ranch. And it would likely happen again.

Yet did Patience think it was her fault? If anyone were to blame, he was. He hadn't been as involved with Evangeline as he should have been. He was realizing that now.

Felicity narrowed her eyes. "I don't know what happened. But it's rattled Patience."

Had it rattled her enough that she'd decided to leave him? Maybe she'd asked Buck to take her away. Maybe by doing so, she'd stepped aside for Felicity.

"You need to talk to her." Felicity spoke firmly.

"But that's just it. She rode off with my ranch foreman earlier in the evening and hasn't come back."

"That can't be. Patience would never run away."

"Under the circumstances? Maybe she would." Fresh shame coursed through him. He hadn't communicated well with her, not only about Evangeline but also about how much he appreciated her. If he'd taken the time to reassure her, maybe she wouldn't have felt the need to leave.

He'd even gone up to her room after the incident, telling himself he only wanted to make sure she was okay. But his longing for her had been strong, and he would have kissed her again, likely more. She'd already been asleep, but maybe he should have awoken her.

Whatever the case, he'd been a fool to wait so long to talk to her. And now he was possibly too late.

"Do you know where she might have gone?" he asked.

"She couldn't have *gone* anywhere. It's not in her nature to do so."

"Nature or not, she didn't come home."

A cool breeze stirred the air, and Felicity shivered.

"Something must have happened."

"Or she decided to leave me." His worst fear was that he'd driven her away and lost her forever.

If he were perfectly honest with himself, that's what he'd done with Honora. He'd driven her away too. She hadn't wanted him to take the trip to America to visit the ranch for his father. She'd wanted him to stay behind and let someone else go. If he had, maybe she wouldn't have turned to another man for companionship.

The truth glared at him, a truth he'd tried to ignore. He'd been a terrible husband then. And he was still terrible. Why had he allowed himself to think this time could be any different?

23

By midmorning, Patience and Buck hadn't returned. And Spencer was going nearly mad with the need to know where they'd gone.

He hadn't slept, had only tossed and turned for the few hours that he'd actually lain down. Most of the night he'd paced, stopping to look out the window at every sound. By dawn, he'd been frazzled and weary.

But he'd arrived at the glaring conclusion that he simply needed to let her go, couldn't send out a search party the way Tex had suggested. He'd obviously hurt her with his callous approach to the marriage. He hadn't cherished her the way he should have. He'd relegated her to being a mother for Evangeline and had withheld his love.

No wonder she'd been ready to leave.

With the soft patter of rain upon the kitchen window, he sipped his coffee and watched the raindrops streak the glass. Evangeline sat on his lap, much too silent, playing with the paper dolls Patience had crafted for her. Ever since Evangeline had awoken to the news that Patience was still gone, she'd clung to him and had been unwilling to move from his side.

He'd decided to stay close to home for the morning. Evangeline needed him now more than ever. And he didn't want her thinking that she was somehow to blame for Patience's leaving.

Patience had been good for Evangeline, had loved her unreservedly. And Evangeline had done the same with Patience. She'd given her heart to her new mother. Now his sweet little girl would have to learn how to survive the heartache.

He supposed if the relationship with Patience must come to an end, it was better to do so now while it was still fairly new rather than later when the severing would be much more painful.

At a call from the ranch yard, he sat forward. Evangeline's hands came to a standstill on one of the colorful paper dresses, and she peered out the window expectantly. "Do you think Mama is back?"

"I'm not sure, darling." He stood and set her on the chair.

Keen longing welled up within him. He missed Patience and wanted her. There was no denying it.

At a knock against the front door, the hope that had

started to swell deflated. It wasn't Patience. She wouldn't knock, would she?

With long strides, he made his way out of the kitchen and down the hallway. As he tossed open the door, he allowed himself another brief instance of hope only to have it crushed again. Felicity stood before him, dripping wet and breathing hard. A horse stood heaving nearby—one she'd likely borrowed from the livery.

She'd insisted on staying in Fairplay last night, taking a room at one of the hotels. According to her calculations, she'd saved up enough of her wages working as Mrs. Bancroft's companion that she could pay for a room for a week or two—until she had the chance to find another living situation.

As he'd assisted her in hauling her belongings over to the hotel, he'd offered her a room at the ranch and the position of Evangeline's nursemaid. But Felicity had remained adamant that Patience would return and be Evangeline's mother again.

He supposed in some ways that Felicity staying at a hotel was better. Then he didn't have to worry about explaining her presence to everyone, especially now that Patience was gone. He didn't want anyone to assume he was replacing Patience with her sister.

Felicity was wearing a bonnet that covered her red hair, but strands had come loose and plastered to her neck and cheek. Her teeth were chattering from the cold. "I take it you haven't heard from Patience yet this morning?"

He shook his head, knowing he should invite her in, but hesitating.

"I heard news this morning that might have something to do with her disappearance." Her eyes were grave, putting him on edge.

"What news?"

"My solicitor sought me out to tell me that this morning Lizette and Gage emptied every last dollar in the bank as well as the gold awaiting transport to Denver."

Lizette and Gage? The cousins who'd taken over the homestead? But why would they do such a thing?

"And they left town on the first stage."

"I don't understand."

"I don't either, but the solicitor says they appeared anxious, were in a hurry to go, and wanted to take with them as much gold as they could carry."

"Maybe they're just going away on a trip."

"Or maybe they're moving away for good?"

He shrugged. "What does this have to do with Patience?"

"If she went to visit them last night, maybe she discovered something about them—something that has them fleeing from town."

Spencer's mind spun suddenly with all the implications.

Felicity's expression darkened. "I've always believed that their showing up now to claim the inheritance was too convenient. But I've never been able to prove anything. I still can't."

"Do you think Patience had some kind of evidence against them?"

"It's certainly worth looking into."

His heart quivered. What if Buck and Patience had gone to confront her cousin but then had come to harm? "The place was deserted last night when I went."

She glanced behind him to Evangeline standing a few feet away, then she dropped her voice. "Do you think Gage and Lizette silenced Patience, perhaps Buck too?"

Silenced? As in killed? Dread began worming its way through him. That possibility was worse than anything he'd conjured. But if Gage and Lizette were nefarious at heart, then what would stop them from murdering anyone who got in their way?

He reached for his oiled cloak on the coat tree and began to don it. "I'm going back over to the homestead."

"I'll go with you." Felicity was already spinning around and striding toward the porch steps.

He bundled Evangeline up and took her to Tex for the saddling lesson. Then within minutes he was riding beside Felicity toward the Courtney homestead.

They traveled in silence, which was fine with him. His thoughts were too self-deprecating to speak aloud. The main strain played over and over in the orchestra already performing in his mind—he'd failed at being a good husband. If he'd been better at it, maybe she would have confided in him instead of Buck. Maybe he could have prevented the two of them from riding off by themselves. Maybe he could have kept everyone from this trouble.

But the truth was that she hadn't wanted to confide in him. And it was no surprise. Why would she have confidence in a husband who hadn't been honest with her from the start of their marriage?

As they rode down the lane toward the house, he was struck as he'd been last night at the shabbiness of the place, even more so in the daylight. Now, with Lizette and Gage having left, would the place fall into more disrepair? Who would live there and take care of the property?

The whole situation was strange indeed.

When they reached the house, Felicity dismounted before he could even halt his horse and was running up the porch steps calling Patience's name almost frantically. The front door was ajar, and she burst into the house, continuing to shout.

Spencer followed more cautiously. He didn't expect to face opposition, but he was terrified of what he would find. He didn't want her to be dead. Not even hurt. Because he loved her with everything within him. Loved her more than he'd thought it possible to love a woman.

As he stepped into the front room, he could see that the interior was as unkempt as the outside. Surely if Gage and Lizette had intended to live in the house for the long term, they would have taken better care of the place. Perhaps they'd planned all along only to stay for a short while. But why?

Felicity's footsteps resounded from the kitchen, then she came back into the front room. "They're not down here." She started up the steps to the bedrooms.

Spencer guessed if Gage and Lizette had wanted to silence Patience and Buck, they wouldn't have done so in the house. Or at the very least, wouldn't have left the bodies lying around.

When Felicity came down a few seconds later, he kept his morbid thoughts to himself.

"I'll check the barn," he offered as they returned to the cold drizzle outside.

She nodded, her face growing paler with every passing moment as if she, too, understood the reality of the situation.

As he crossed the yard, the image of Patience standing in the barn door with the kitten rushed to the front of his memories of her. Even that first night he'd been smitten with her. He'd been smitten all along, every day and every minute she'd been his wife. He'd just been too stubborn to admit it.

The barn door was open, and the stench of manure

and urine filled the air. If Gage and Lizette hadn't taken care of the house, then he guessed they hadn't been responsible with the barn or the livestock either.

He stepped inside and paused to let his eyes adjust to the darkness of the cloudy day. The soft nicker of a horse greeted him. He crossed to the stall and froze at the sight that met him. Buck's gelding. And the horse in the next stall over was the one Patience had been riding when she'd left with Buck.

"Devil it." He slapped a hand against the top post, the despair mounting so quickly it choked him. Perhaps he'd been holding out hope that the two had gotten away, had gone someplace to wait out the danger. Even Patience running off with Buck as her lover was better than what this meant.

It meant they'd been captured, maybe killed, and their bodies thrown into the woods or the nearby creek.

He'd have to head back to his ranch, round up a posse of men, and spread out for a hunt. Even if slim, there might be a chance that the two were just injured.

He wouldn't stop looking until he found them.

24

Patience hadn't moved from the crate in hours. She stood with her back against the damp earth, shivering and stiff and weary. And the shoulder that Gage had hit with his gun burned with pain. She guessed he'd broken a bone—perhaps her collarbone. She'd dozed off and on throughout the long, cold night. But she'd been too overcome by fear and pain to rest much.

The cloudy day outside didn't provide much light, but it was enough that she could see the ground, shelves, and Buck crouched on another overturned crate beside her with two dead rattlers on the floor near him.

During the night, he'd managed to kill them even in the dark, swiping them up with his bare hands, snapping them, and breaking their necks in one swift move. He'd said there was nothing to it, that every good cowhand could kill a rattler.

Of course, such skills were useful only if the rattler

came out of hiding. And the third rattler hadn't yet made its move to strike at them. When she'd questioned how Gage had had the rattlers, Buck had assured her that good crooks sometimes kept the deadly creatures on hand for assassination occasions like this.

The plunking of rain against the door overhead made it difficult for them to hear the rattle. But Buck had remained vigilant, hadn't slept all night. When she'd offered to watch for the snake so he could sleep, he'd shaken his head.

"You're sure?" she asked again. "I can take a turn watching."

"No offense." His tone was dry, almost bitter. "After the deep pile of manure you got us in, I don't trust you."

She let her head drop and her shoulders sag. She could admit, since the moment they'd arrived at the homestead, she'd created a disaster. And he was right. No one should trust her. She'd keep everyone safer if she stayed single and childless and lived a simple life by herself.

All the more reason not to return to Spencer once she and Buck were free. Surely they would be set free. Someone had to come looking for them soon. But why would anyone think to check the cellar?

She sighed again, as she had a dozen times over recent hours.

A woman's voice seemed to waft in the yard outside.

Was it Lucy? Or someone else?

She stilled herself and listened again, trying to distinguish anything past the patter of rain. "I think I heard someone."

Buck stared up at the hatch as if he was trying to see through it.

"Should I bang against the door, just in case?"

"Go ahead. Reckon it can't hurt."

She reached her arm up and winced. Then she switched to her other arm and pounded against the plank. "Help! Anyone! We're down here!" She slammed her fist several times harder.

Holding her breath, she waited, prayed someone would hear.

But after a minute of only the rain, she sagged against the wall.

Buck was silent.

Again, a woman's voice seemed to be calling. For her. Was Felicity out there?

This time Patience started banging with all her strength and yelling as loudly as she could. "Felicity! It's me! I'm here! Felicity!"

A moment later, a woman's voice came from outside the cellar. "Patience?"

"Yes. Buck and I are locked up here in the cellar."

"They're here!" Felicity called to someone, relief ringing in her voice.

"Patience? Buck?" A moment later, Spencer's voice sounded from above the door. "Are you in there?"

A sob welled up inside Patience, and she captured it behind her hand. Spencer had come. He'd been looking for her.

"We're here." Buck still hadn't moved, remaining as vigilant as before.

"Are you hurt?" Felicity called.

"We're fine," Buck responded. "But there's still one more rattlesnake on the loose."

"Rattlesnake?" Spencer's voice radiated worry.

"Gage dumped three of them down here."

The chain on the door began to rattle. "We have to find the key." Felicity spoke with familiar passion.

For what felt like forever, the two disappeared, likely searching for the key. Finally the rattling of the door above signaled their return.

"They must have taken the key with them," Felicity said. "We'll have to break down the door."

"Stand back out of the way," Spencer instructed. "I'm going to hack through the wood."

"We ain't got much room." Buck straightened as much as he could. "Go easy."

In the next second, the blade of an axe sliced through the wood, splintering it. After several more hard chops with bits of wood raining down, Spencer had created a hole big enough that they could see Felicity's face peeking through.

"You're okay?" she asked.

"We are now," Buck responded before Patience could.

The axe pulverized the wood until, at last, Spencer bent and began to rip parts away with his gloved hands. When he finally stopped and looked down, his gaze was frantic as it landed upon her.

Though the cloudy day obscured her from seeing him as fully as she wanted, she took him in eagerly—his darkly shadowed chin and jaw, his slanted brows, his forehead furrowed under the brim of his Stetson.

"You're sure you're unharmed?" he asked.

"My shoulder hurts from where Gage hit me with his gun."

Spencer's lips pressed together, and anger hardened his features.

If the broken collarbone was the worst injury that came from the occasion, then she couldn't complain. They could have easily been bitten by the rattlesnakes. Or trapped in the cellar for days.

Rainwater dripping from his long coat, Spencer reached down both hands for her. She tried to latch on, but at the movement of her injured arm, she couldn't hold back a cry of pain.

Spencer's brows dipped deeper. "Help hoist her up, Buck."

With Buck's help from down low and Spencer's careful pulling from up top, she slipped through the jagged hole. Spencer hoisted her to her feet and steadied her. As he did so, she got lost in his eyes, the concern there engulfing her and making her remember everything about him that she loved.

She loved this man, and she wanted to throw herself against him, wrap her arms around him, and just hold him. He was so strong and faithful and kind and everything she could ever want in a husband.

If only she could be what he needed in a wife.

But no. She'd made up her mind. He'd married her by mistake, and now she needed to set him free from being with her.

He seemed to hesitate, his hold on her arms wavering, as if he couldn't quite make up his mind whether he wanted to hug her.

Before he was forced to choose, she took a step back. In the next instant, Felicity was reaching for her and drawing her into an embrace. She fell into her sister and let the tears have release. Tears of relief at being rescued. Tears of gratefulness at surviving. Tears of fondness for this dear sister who'd found her and Buck. But also tears of sorrow and regret and pain at having to say goodbye to Spencer. This had to be their parting.

When Buck was free from the cellar, he was already rattling off the details of all that had transpired to lead them to the homestead, as well as what had happened when they'd arrived.

"So they were frauds?" Felicity rubbed Patience's arms.

"Lucy's not our cousin." Patience glanced around at the yard, taking in the dilapidated state as she had yesterday when she'd arrived—the overgrown garden and grass, untended livestock, and the roaming chickens. "The place is still rightfully ours."

Felicity was following her gaze. "It's going to take some work to clean it up. But I'll manage."

"What about your work with Mrs. Bancroft?"

"I quit last night."

Goodness gracious. They had a lot of catching up to do. But at least they could live in their home again. "I'll stay and help you."

"No, you belong with Spencer. I can see it. Everyone can see it."

At Felicity's pronouncement, Spencer halted his conversation with Buck. His stormy green-brown eyes latched onto Patience. What was he thinking? That she was too much of a hassle? That he wanted to be done with their marriage?

She couldn't read the answers. If he felt that they belonged together, wouldn't he invite her to come back to the ranch, tell her that he wanted her? Something?

Instead, he stood stiffly and said nothing.

"I finally discovered you married me by mistake, Spencer." The rain was falling harder, running down her face and making her even colder. "I wasn't the one you expected. It's only fair that I allow you to choose who you want."

A part of her longed for him to cross to her, pull her into his arms, and tell her she was the one he wanted. But another part of her resisted. She couldn't forget that he'd be better off without her.

"I'll be living here with Felicity." She lifted her chin, trying to keep herself from collapsing while her world crumbled around her.

He nodded curtly. "I'll have someone bring your things by later."

Then he was agreeing? That easily? A sob rose into her throat. She clutched at her arms and started toward the back door of the house, needing to get away before she betrayed herself and raced after him, begging him to take her back with him.

Once again, he didn't say anything to stop her. But his silence spoke loudly enough.

25

Spencer rode back to the ranch without speaking a word. With every mile he put between himself and Patience, his heart ripped out a little more.

What was he doing leaving her behind?

Buck had been quiet for the cold, wet ride. His misery and weariness rolled off him in waves. The ordeal had been harrowing, and Buck had done it out of the goodness of his heart to help Patience and Felicity. He hadn't been looking for anything in return.

The least Spencer could do was thank him.

As the ranch house and barns came into view across the last span of open prairie, Spencer brought his horse to a halt. Buck reined in and bumped up the brim of his hat to give Spencer his attention.

"Thank you for taking care of her. I'm indebted to you." He couldn't keep the emotion from sneaking into his gratitude. When Felicity had called to him that she'd found Patience, he'd been striding toward his horse ready to ride back to the ranch to gather up a group of men to start a manhunt. He'd nearly collapsed to his knees under the weight of his relief in learning Patience was alive.

Buck held his gaze. "Reckon Felicity hit the bull's-eye."

"About what?"

"Everyone can see you belong with Patience."

Spencer pressed his lips together, having no intention of discussing his relationship with his foreman.

But of course, Buck didn't take the hint and continued. "From the first day you brought her back to the ranch, you've taken to her like honeysuckle to a front porch."

Spencer knew he'd *taken to her*. But he cocked his brow anyway. What was Buck's point?

"Don't know why you're here chawing with me and not back there"—he nodded his head north toward the Courtney homestead—"fighting for that woman."

Spencer had just asked himself the same question. What was he doing? Why was he letting her slip away? He didn't even want to begin picturing the future without her in it. The very thought was too morbid, too bleak, too unfathomable.

But how could he fight for her when he'd driven her away? And even if he won her back this time, what was to stop him from inadvertently driving her away the next time issues came up?

"Well?" Buck waited, hands resting on his thighs as if he had all day to sit and dole out relationship advice.

"It's complicated."

"From where I sit, it ain't any more complicated than getting your sorry self back over there and convincing her you love her and want her to stay with you."

"Maybe she deserves someone better than me." The words slipped out before he could stop them.

Buck snorted. "Yep. Most women do deserve better. That's why it's our job each and every day to show them they're something mighty special."

Convincing her that he loved her. Showing her she was special. Could he do that?

He stared ahead, seeing only her. Her beauty, her smile, her blue eyes wide upon him with interest and invitation.

She'd come into his life unexpectedly, but she'd been the best thing that had ever happened to him. He could easily acknowledge that.

It was almost as if she'd awoken him from a deep slumber. Instead of walking around in the dark, he was seeing more clearly. She hadn't said anything to him, hadn't condemned him, hadn't nagged him. But somehow, in the light of her kindness and sweetness, he'd begun to see how much more he needed to do for Evangeline, how he could be a better father, how he could love his daughter more completely.

He let his gaze linger over the house. Before she'd arrived, everything had been sterile and barren. But she left splashes of color and joy in her wake wherever she went. Even in the drizzle, the signs of her were everywhere. The brightly painted steps, the colorful flowerpots, the little flags and chimes and painted rocks. The inside of the house was the same way. She'd brought life to every corner. And she'd filled their home with her love, holding nothing back, always giving with no thought of receiving anything in return.

Why hadn't he done the same? Why had he held himself back?

His head dropped, and he released a groan. "Devil it. I've made a royal muddle of things, haven't I?"

Buck's hand clamped against his arm. "Reckon half of life's a muddle and the other half is trying to make up for it."

Could he make up for this? He wasn't sure.

In the distance, Evangeline had stepped off the porch and was starting to run toward him. Tex was following behind her more slowly.

Even though Evangeline would be relieved to learn Patience was safe, she'd be devastated to discover her mama wasn't coming back.

Did he have it within his power to keep from hurting his daughter and causing her heartache? If he went to

Patience and asked her to return for Evangeline, he suspected Patience would do it, even at great personal cost to herself. That was how Patience was.

But the truth was, he couldn't do that to her. That wouldn't be fair. She deserved everything. She deserved a man who spent each and every day showing her how special she truly was, just like Buck said. And a man who made up for his muddles.

He swallowed hard against the familiar protest rising within him that accused him of not being that kind of man. From today onward, he had to change that.

He stuck out his hand toward Buck. "You're a good fellow."

Buck took the offer and shook firmly. "So are you."

Spencer gathered his reins and nudged his horse forward. "Guess I better get busy. I've got to come up with a plan for how to convince my wife to come back home and let me love her like she deserves."

"Now that's what I'm talking about." Buck's call followed him. "You go and get her."

Spencer suspected it would be more complicated than simply going and getting her. But he'd never turned down a challenge. And wouldn't start now.

As he crossed the distance toward Evangeline, the little girl raced forward, her hair unbrushed, her clothing the same from yesterday, her face a mask of worry. Without Patience in their lives bringing them her love and life, they were both wilting. They needed her.

He needed her.

Several feet from Evangeline, he halted his horse and hopped down in one fluid motion, just in time for her to launch herself into his arms.

He gathered her close and held her a moment before she began to wiggle from his embrace. "How's Mama?"

"She's fine and safe."

"Where is she?"

How did he answer Evangeline without raising her hope too high? How did he keep his own hope from rising too high?

"She's not here yet. But I hope she will be soon." Maybe he had to start by being humble and admitting his mistakes. He knelt in front of her, holding her hands, the drizzle falling over them both. "I have to show your mama that I love her better, just like I have to show you better."

"You do?"

"Yes. I haven't done a very good job of that. But I want you to know—and I want your mama to know too—that I love you both more than anything else."

Evangeline's blue eyes widened, eyes so much like Patience's. For the first time, he didn't see Honora and all the horrible memories when he looked at his daughter. Instead, he saw Patience and the hope of a brighter future together.

And now it was time for him to figure out exactly how to make that future happen.

26

Patience tried to be happy she was back at the homestead. But she wasn't able to convince herself. And from everything Felicity was saying, she clearly wasn't convincing her sister either.

"You can't give up so easily." Felicity bustled about the kitchen, now thoroughly tidied after hours of cleaning.

Patience stood at the center worktable, the paring knife idle in her hand, stacks of shriveled vegetables waiting to be salvaged, having dried out over the weeks of not being watered.

Was her life like the vegetables? Did she have the ability to salvage the good out of the bad? She wanted to, but the pile seemed overwhelming.

Felicity removed a lid from a pot on the stove and began to stir the sauce inside. "You need to go talk with him."

She didn't have to ask Felicity to clarify who *him* was. She knew.

More than anything, she wanted to ride over to the ranch. She'd thought of doing so at least a dozen times yesterday after Spencer had left. She'd thought of doing so at least a dozen times during her restless night. And she'd also thought of doing so at least a dozen times already this morning.

But she couldn't. "He doesn't want me, Felicity. And there's nothing I can do to change that."

"He wants you." Felicity spoke the words so confidently that for a moment Patience allowed herself a measure of hope. After all, she'd been wrong many times before in reading people, even reading Spencer. What if he wanted her and she just hadn't been able to see it?

It didn't matter. Even if he did want her, she was giving him the opportunity to find a better wife, someone he actually chose and not a wife he'd gained as a result of a misunderstanding.

Her cheeks flushed again as they did every time she thought about how she'd stepped in and married him when he'd been expecting Felicity. How daft could a person be to miss all the clues the way she had?

She set the paring knife down and untied the apron covering one of Felicity's gowns. The borrowed garment was slightly tight, but it was sufficing until her trunks and bags arrived. Spencer had indicated he'd have them delivered yesterday. But no one had come all day.

She didn't understand how that was possible, since she and Felicity had gone to town at least twice. On the first trip, they'd retrieved Felicity's belongings from the hotel room where she'd stayed the previous night. And they'd also visited Dr. Steele, who'd examined Patience's collarbone and didn't believe it was broken. On the second ride into town, they'd met with their solicitor to discover what, if anything, was left of their finances.

During the meeting, they'd gleaned more information about all that had transpired with Gage and Lucy. Apparently the solicitor had realized something was wrong when the couple had rushed into town not long after locking Patience and Buck in the cellar and knocked on his door after dark, telling him they were leaving on a trip and demanding he give them access to all of the inheritance.

He hadn't allowed them inside his residence and had insisted they wait for the morning to meet him at the bank. Not only had their demands been alarming, but so had the fact that they'd had their bags with them and indicated they were staying at a hotel room in town.

Already having doubts based upon the interactions with the couple over the past weeks, the solicitor had gone to the bank early and spoken with the administrator, who had agreed with the plan to only keep a portion of the money and gold in the Courtney name and to remove the rest into a temporary account until they could investigate further into the matter.

Thus, though Gage and Lucy had left with much more than they deserved, they hadn't stolen everything. Even so, Felicity had reported the couple to the sheriff's office, hoping that eventually the two would be caught and brought to justice before being able to prey on anyone else.

If only Felicity had been the one to come out to the house and confront Gage and Lucy. She likely would have come up with a plan to have them arrested before they could escape.

At least the crooks had left behind the family Bible along with their Uncle John's letters to his wife in California. She and Felicity had read through the correspondences to discover the fuller story of all that had happened.

From what they could piece together, their uncle had left his wife Wilma in California with the promise of paying for her to move to Colorado once he had a place ready for her. Apparently, after getting the homestead, he'd lovingly decorated the place for her. But then in her last letter, it was clear she'd been too sick to travel and that she knew she was dying.

There had been no mention of a daughter. Patience and Felicity concluded that somehow Gage had forged the name into the family Bible. Or perhaps he'd taken out any letters that referenced Lizette and destroyed them.

Maybe they'd never know.

Whatever the case, Patience wished she hadn't been so reckless with Gage and Lucy.

She sighed out her frustration at herself, then set the apron on the table. The morning sunshine was beckoning to her. If only it could cheer her heart. "You don't mind if I go out and do more yard work, do you? The day is perfect for it."

Felicity glanced to the pile of vegetables, to the paring knife, then back to Patience. "Is this your way of telling me that you'd rather not talk about Spencer?"

"You know I'm not smart enough to come up with excuses."

"Don't be so disparaging."

"It's true."

"It is not."

"Yes, it is. I'm too scattered."

Felicity opened her mouth as though to continue the argument but then hesitated before she next spoke. "Why do you think that about yourself?"

"Mother told me I was too scattered and that no man would want me for a wife." As soon as the words were out, she wished she could pull them back in. No doubt everyone in the family had heard Mother scold her enough that the words weren't a surprise.

"Maybe she said that when you were younger, but she didn't mean it."

"Yes. She did."

Felicity paused in stirring the liquid inside the pot, a fierce frown forming. "Even if she did feel that way, you can't let her voice define who you are."

Patience didn't know how to respond to that piece of advice.

"I loved our mother, don't mistake that." Felicity's tone turned firm. "But she had high expectations for each of us and was difficult to please."

"For you too?"

"Yes, for me too."

They'd rarely discussed their parents, and when they did, they were always respectful. It felt almost sacrilegious to speak of their mother's faults.

"The truth is, Patience, you're beautiful both inside and out. Whatever Mother said was wrong, because even if you are scattered and distractible at times, you're kind and loving and sweet. And those qualities matter more than anything else."

"Thank you. That's kind of you to say—"

"Every man in the county has secretly admired you and wanted you for a wife. You're always just too caught up in your creations to notice."

Patience flushed at her sister's bold words. "But the only man who matters wants you instead." Once the words were out, she clamped a hand over her mouth.

Felicity just grinned and shook her head. "No, when I

told him of your plan to have me step in and take your place, he told me he wasn't interested in having anyone but you."

"He said that?" She couldn't keep the surprise from ringing in her tone.

"Is it really that hard to believe a man would want you?" Felicity had resumed her stirring. "If it is, maybe you need to work on loving and accepting yourself the same way that you do everyone else."

"Maybe." Patience watched Felicity for a moment longer before heading outside. Felicity's words echoed in her head as she used the scythe to cut back the weeds growing along the perimeter of the house and in the flowerbeds. They echoed in her head when she realized a front shutter above one of the flowerbeds was hanging loose. And they echoed in her head when she went into the barn to get a hammer to fix the shutter.

Once in the barn, the words continued to echo as she used the hammer to fix a broken slat of the wagon and then fashion a simple feedbox for the goats. She wished for her art supplies so she could paint beautiful designs all over the box. But she'd already resigned herself to waiting.

As she hammered the last nail and gently rolled her sore shoulder, she paused at the sound of wagon wheels rumbling down the path toward the house. Were Spencer's men finally coming to deliver her things? Maybe she wouldn't have to wait overly long to paint again after all.

Even as that thought surged through her, so did frustration. She didn't want her things here. She wanted them at the ranch. *She* wanted to be at the ranch.

As much as she loved Felicity and had relished the opportunity to catch up with her sister and hear all about her nightmarish experience with Mrs. Bancroft, her heart pounded out the need to be with Spencer and Evangeline and her new life with them.

Maybe if she stayed in the barn and hid, the men would go back and tell Spencer they couldn't deliver her trunks and bags. Most likely they would just carry her things inside and deposit them with Felicity before leaving.

Regardless, Patience couldn't make herself walk out of the barn. The hurt and disappointment welled up too deeply. If Spencer had told Felicity that he wasn't interested in having anybody but her, then why was he bringing back her belongings?

She paced, twisting her beautiful wedding band. He'd have to come and get it from her, wouldn't he? He'd have no choice but to face her eventually. At that point, what should she do? Throw herself at him? Tell him she wanted to be with him? Admit that she'd let her insecurities keep her from staying with him?

Because that was the truth. She might not ever be able to get her mother's voice out of her head. But maybe if she let the echo of Felicity's statement grow louder, it would eventually drown out the negative.

Suddenly cold, she hugged her arms to her chest and plopped down on the nearest hay bale.

One of the kittens—the orange tabby—rubbed against her legs. They'd grown while she'd been away but were still petite, likely hadn't gotten enough nourishment. She scooped up the little fellow and scratched behind its ears. Immediately she was rewarded with loud purring.

"Aw, you sweet thing," she whispered.

As heavy footsteps crunched in the gravel outside the barn door, she buried her face in the kitten's soft fur. One of the ranch hands was obviously seeking her out, and the kitten wouldn't hide her the way she wished it could. But she felt safer regardless.

The footsteps entered the barn and then stopped abruptly.

She waited for the man to speak instructions of some kind. But silence dragged on for so long that she finally glanced up. Instead of a ranch hand, Spencer stood in the doorway. Outlined by the morning sunlight, he'd never been more handsome, his muscular body as imposing and statuesque as always. He'd taken off his hat and held it in his hand, and his woodsy brown hair was combed back neatly, as if he'd taken the time specifically to look his best.

He always looked his best to her, even when he was at his worst, like when he'd come home the week he'd been haying—full of sweat and dust and with bits of hay sticking to him. Even then, she'd still thought he was incredibly good-looking.

"Hello, Patience." He didn't move from the doorway, but his eyes roved over her, and he seemed to be taking her in with the same measure that she was him. "May I come in?"

She set the kitten gently down and then pushed up to her feet. What if he'd come for the ring? She couldn't just hand it over without trying to salvage their marriage. But what could she say?

"How's Evangeline?" Her heart had been aching for the little girl. She could only imagine how frightened and worried the child had been to learn of everything that had happened. And now to lose her mama?

"She misses you."

"I miss her too. Very much." Unexpected tears stung her eyes. She had to say something before she started crying. She twisted the ring again. "I know why you came."

"You do?" His attention dropped to her fingers and the ring.

Quickly she hid her hands behind her back. Yet even as she did so, she forced herself to slowly slip the ring off. What good would come of making him ask her for it? More humiliation for both of them?

She took a deep breath, then thrust her hand out. Her

fist was closed, and for a moment she thought maybe she'd have to physically pry her own fingers open. Then, with a strength she hadn't realized she had, she opened her hand and let the jewel rest in her palm.

His sights dropped to the ring and then swung back to her face. "You're giving me back the ring?"

"It's not mine to keep, especially when you'll need it again."

"I don't plan to need it again."

"You'll find someone else who will cherish it." She had to work hard to keep her voice from cracking. He was too handsome and masculine and divine. He could easily find another woman to marry.

"I don't want anyone else to cherish it."

"I don't see why they wouldn't, not when it's so lovely."

He watched her for a moment as though trying to understand what she was saying.

What was she saying? She didn't even know for herself.

One of his brows quirked.

The movement, even though small, was so attractive that she couldn't keep her pulse from racing forward with a surge of desire. She loved so many things about him, even his questioning eyebrow tics.

His other brow rose, and he began to cross to her.

Was he going to take the ring?

27

She was most definitely trying to end their relationship.

The air in Spencer's lungs was growing shorter with every passing moment. It felt as if a noose was closing around him and about to draw him up and hang him if he didn't act.

The only thing that was keeping him from grabbing the ring and running out of the barn like a wounded animal with his tail tucked between his legs was the look in her eyes. She was peering at him as though he was a sugary confection that she wanted to taste.

That had to mean something, didn't it?

As he reached her outstretched hand, he didn't even bother looking down at it. Instead he kept his gaze locked with hers. He'd come here to win her back. And even if she was returning the ring, he had to tell her what he'd rehearsed throughout the long night.

He studied the jewel-toned blue of her eyes, her long

lashes, and her heavy lids that never failed to make him think of lying next to her in bed. But not at this moment. He couldn't let his thoughts wander there.

Yes, her eyes were certainly conveying a message, one filled with longing.

Was this, then, another mix-up moment? Were they both making assumptions without really communicating clearly? Based on previous mishaps, he guessed he'd landed on what was happening. But even if he was wrong and even if she rejected him anyway, he had to state very clearly and succinctly why he was there so that she couldn't misunderstand him at all.

He drew himself up, trying to gain a measure of fortitude to press on. As he did so, he couldn't help but notice that her outstretched hand wavered.

Gently he closed her fingers around the wedding ring and moved her hand back to her side. "The reason I don't plan to need the ring again is because . . ."

She inhaled a trembling breath. Was it dread for what he was about to say?

He pushed aside the thought and forged onward. "I want you to keep it."

Her eyes rounded and filled with confusion. "I wouldn't feel right about keeping it if we're not married."

He was getting this all wrong. He had to just say what he'd planned to. In the next moment, he lowered himself onto one knee in front of her and gently captured the hand that wasn't holding the ring.

He brought it to his lips and kissed her knuckles.

This time the desire that flashed in her eyes was unmistakable.

Emboldened, he brushed another soft kiss against her hand. "The other day you told me that I should choose who I want. And I choose you, Patience. It's always been you, and I was just too much of a fool to admit it."

She began to shake her head.

Was she rejecting him? He couldn't let her. He tossed aside the speech he'd prepared and instead said the one thing he hoped would communicate his feelings the best. "I love you."

She stilled, her eyes widening.

"I love you and want you to be my wife forever." Maybe his declaration hadn't been as poetic and grand as he'd rehearsed, but hopefully his words left no room for confusion or misunderstanding.

She opened her mouth to respond but then just as quickly closed it.

He reached for her other hand, extracted the ring, and then slid it back down her finger. "I don't ever want to give you another reason to take this off."

She studied the ring back on her finger as though she couldn't believe it was there. "Are you sure, Spencer? I lost track of Evangeline, and she could have died because of me." Her eyes welled with tears.

Without releasing his clasp on her hand, he stood. "That wasn't the first occasion Evangeline rode off on her pony to find me."

"It wasn't?"

"She's done it other times too. I should have warned you that she was hard to manage."

"She's not hard, Spencer. She just misses you when you're gone for too long."

Evangeline missed him when he was gone? Was that why she'd ridden out all those times?

"I've noticed she's much calmer and less anxious when you spend some time with her every day, even if just a little." Patience's voice didn't hold any condemnation, only gentleness.

Just one of the many, many traits he loved about her. "So, you see. Her leaving the house unsupervised is my fault. Not yours."

"I still hold myself responsible."

"But you're not. Maybe Evangeline has just been afraid that she'll lose me like she lost her mother."

Her gaze widened at the mention of Honora. He supposed he'd made it quite clear that he didn't like talking about her. But today, he had to do it. "I have likewise been afraid, perhaps unwittingly so, that I might lose again too. That's partly why I rode away yesterday like a fool, because I was scared."

She squeezed his arm as though to excuse him.

But he couldn't excuse himself. He had to tell her the whole truth. "When I was visiting in America, Honora developed a friendship with a neighboring nobleman, one of my childhood chums." He paused, expecting the pain that usually pierced him at the thought of the betrayal, not only by his wife but by one of his closest friends. And although he could feel an ache in his chest—maybe always would—the sharp pain was no longer there.

He pressed on, needing to get out the rest of the sordid story. "Their friendship developed into more, and when I returned, I walked in on them sleeping together in our bed."

Patience didn't gasp or act shocked or anything. Instead, she kept her hand on his arm, steady, comforting, and lending him her strength.

"Honora told me she wanted a divorce. But I wanted to try to make things work, especially for Evangeline. Honora left me anyway, and a few days later, she died after miscarrying his baby." He'd already made plans at that point to return to the ranch in America. The scandal had made it certain. "I didn't think I'd ever be able to trust again. But I'm learning. I hope you'll bear with me, as I still have work to do."

"Of course, we all do. And thank you for telling me about your wife. You didn't have to."

"I needed to. For my sake."

She nodded, her eyes full of such honesty. In fact, she

had so much honesty she hadn't been able to lie the previous day to save her life, according to Buck.

As if still uncertain what to think of all that had transpired, she cast her eyes down to the hay. The kitten she'd been holding—again, so adorably—was rolling in the hay at her feet.

He tapped at her chin, forcing her eyes back up to his, but at the same time his fingers lingered, his need to touch her so strong he couldn't pull away. "You're the best mother for Evangeline I could ever ask for, better than Honora by far. And I mean that with all my heart."

"But I never say the right thing, always manage to mix things up."

"I don't mind. The misunderstandings are teaching me that I need to be clearer in sharing how I really feel."

"But I'm messy and easily distracted and get caught up in fanciful projects . . ."

"You bring beauty and life to everything around you." Maybe he would get to say part of his speech after all. "When you left, all I could see was your creative touch everywhere, both inside and outside of my home. I didn't know all that I was missing until you came and showed me. And now I can't go back to the way it was. I want you to come home with me and continue to fill my home with your beauty and life. And in return, I promise to love you every day and make you feel so special that hopefully, one day, you'll eventually be able to love me too."

Her lips trembled and the tears spilled over and ran down her cheeks.

Had he said something wrong? He brushed his thumb across her tears. "Don't cry, darling."

"Oh, Spencer." More tears cascaded down her perfect skin. "I won't eventually be able to love you."

"It's okay if you don't." He was going to try hard to win her. Every day. Just as Buck had said. "I'll still love you. I won't ever stop."

"No." Her expression grew earnest. "That's not what I meant."

"Tell me that you'll come back home with me and let me love you. That's all that matters to me."

"No, Spencer."

"No?"

"I mean, yes, I'll come home with you. But no—" She released an exasperated breath. Then her gaze fixed on his mouth. Before he knew what was happening, she lifted on her toes and pressed her lips to his.

Was this her answer?

He didn't stop to ask. He took the sweet offering, letting his mouth fuse to hers in response. Gently, delicately. He stroked as softly as she was, letting her set the pace, since she was the one who'd initiated.

Her lips seemed to savor each part of his mouth, starting at his bottom lip, moving to the corner and gliding around. The friction was heavenly. It was almost as if he was one of her creations that she was sketching and brushing and bringing to life. And as she finished the first layer, she started again with bolder and firmer strokes.

When her arms slid up and wrapped around his neck, he gave himself permission to slip his arms around her waist in return. He wanted to draw her against him. But again, he allowed her to move at her will.

Her fingers tentatively grazed his hair at the back of his neck, and the barest touch released a blaze of heat to every part of his body—a heat he could no longer ignore.

And this time when she pressed in even harder, he couldn't hold back. He groaned, dragging her flush so that he could feel her heart beating against his. At the same time, he took the kiss to a whole new medium, one she probably hadn't known existed. But she seemed to eagerly follow him, tangling and tasting, as if once again she was creating something beautiful and breathtaking.

His body filled with a life he couldn't ever remember feeling before. Her kiss had brought him that life, had filled him with love. Her love.

She loved him. She hadn't said the words. But that's what she'd been trying to communicate through her kiss—that she wouldn't eventually love him. She already did.

He broke away suddenly.

She gave a soft cry of protest and clung to his neck.

He couldn't keep from smiling. "I'm hoping we can do more of that later. Much, much more."

Her eyes were hazy, half-lidded, and her lips swollen. Too tempting for him. "I don't want to wait until later." Her whisper was filled with wanting and hunger, so much that he couldn't help himself.

He bent and tasted her again, and the intimate tangle started anew with another kiss that rivaled the creation of the world itself, setting into place the moon and stars and sun.

Her passion was proving to be unrivaled, a passion he was looking forward to experiencing in full very soon. But for now, he had to make sure she understood all he was offering her.

Again, he dragged himself from the kiss, only to have her whimper and set him ablaze with the tiny sound. He would have dipped in and lost himself in another kiss except that if he did, he suspected the fire would consume him and he might not be able to stop with just kissing.

Instead, he drew her against his chest, cradling the back of her head with his hand, stroking her hair and kissing her temple.

"Spencer?" she whispered, her voice breathless and drenched with desire.

He closed his eyes and fought against his own need. "Hmmm?"

"I love you already."

The threads of her whisper wrapped up around his heart like a ribbon tying together a gift. The kiss had been gift enough for him, but her words only made it all the better. "I know."

"You do?"

"Let's just say your kisses communicate very clearly how you feel."

"They do?" Her question was tinged with embarrassment.

"Yes. I hope that you'll communicate that way with me often."

She snuggled against him, as if his answer had pleased her. "How often?"

Multiple times a day? Every time they were together? How honest should he be? He went for a tame answer. "As often as is comfortable for you."

"Then you have no limit to this type of communication?"

"Absolutely none."

"Good." Her voice was shy but contained the hint of a smile.

A thrill wound through him. "Does that mean I've convinced you?"

"Convinced me?"

"To come back home and let me show you how much I love you every day for the rest of my life."

She pulled back then and peered up at him with a

wide, beautiful smile lighting her face. "I could use more convincing."

"You could?" He couldn't contain his surprise.

"Yes, often."

As he studied her face and the light in her eyes, he let his worry fall away. Instead, he mimicked her from a moment ago. "How often?"

"As often as is comfortable for you."

He grinned, then bent and stole a hard but short kiss. "I'll be convincing you all the time, then," he growled against her mouth.

"Then our arrangement will work out perfectly."

And he intended to make sure it did.

Patience could think of nothing but getting Spencer alone and kissing him again. She was embarrassed with how badly she wanted it.

As he guided her up the front steps of the ranch house with her eyes blindfolded, she wished she could pull the bandana down, throw her body against his, and kiss him the rest of the day. But Evangeline walked on the other side of her, clutching her hand so tightly that Patience had a feeling the girl might never let her go.

"You're going to love the surprise, Mama." Evangeline also hadn't stopped talking since the moment Patience had arrived at the ranch a short while ago. When Evangeline had seen the wagon rolling toward the house, she'd hopped out of the swing, where Tex had been pushing her, and she'd raced faster than a doe across the yard, tears coursing down her cheeks.

As Spencer had stopped the wagon, Patience hadn't

waited for his help. Instead, she'd scrambled down eagerly and embraced the child with a fierce hug, her own tears falling again.

They'd walked hand in hand the rest of the distance to the house, with Tex welcoming her back and even Buck giving her a nod from where he stood in the corral watching them.

Spencer had driven the wagon up to the house and had Tex help him unload the two trunks that were in the wagon bed and carry them inside.

Before she and Spencer had left Felicity and the homestead, Spencer had assured her that all of her belongings were still at the ranch. But he'd brought two trunks with him filled with items that he'd intended to use to bribe her to return with him if his speech hadn't worked.

Of course his speech had worked. And his kisses. Just his coming had been enough. And she'd told him that when he'd shown her the trunks. But he'd quirked his brow and said, "I'm desperately in love with you and want you to know it."

When she'd asked to see what was inside, he'd insisted that she had to follow his original plan and wait to open them when she got back to the ranch.

During the short ride, she'd debated scooting over on the bench and sitting right next to him so that she could lean in and kiss him. But she hadn't wanted to seem too anxious for more kisses, even though she was. She'd also considered coming up with an excuse and asking him to stop during the ride so that she could tell him she was ready for more of his convincing kisses.

But she'd held herself back. And now she was glad she had. For Evangeline's sake. The child had likely been waiting anxiously, ready to hop on her pony and ride over to see what was taking them so long.

"Papa and Tex and a few other fellows and I sure did spend a lot of time yesterday getting everything ready."

"Yesterday?" Patience asked the question of Spencer, leaning into his solid arm that was brushing against hers.

"Yes, by the time I got back to the ranch, I already knew I'd made a mistake leaving you behind. And I was determined to right the wrong."

"If you'd come back yesterday and worked at convincing me then like you did today, I would have returned immediately."

"Is that so?" His voice lilted with mirth.

"Yes." A flush of warmth spread through her, as it did every time she thought of the kisses she'd shared with Spencer in the barn. She'd been making a fool of herself again, had been bumbling in expressing herself and had feared she'd ruin things for good. So she'd done the only thing she'd known to tell him how she really felt. She'd kissed him.

She still couldn't believe she'd been so bold. But she'd

done it. She'd planned to give him a soft kiss to let him know that she loved him in return. But somehow it had turned into so much more.

Goodness gracious. She wanted to fan her face just thinking about the passion that had ignited inside her. Being with him like that had turned her into a flame that could permanently light up a dozen oil lantern globes. And she'd been burning ever since.

Now, as the door squeaked open and she entered into the front hallway, she leaned against Spencer again, unable to get enough of his solid arms. She wanted those arms to wrap around her again, wanted to lay her head against his hard chest, wanted to simply bask in the delight that he loved her and had chosen her to be his wife forever.

He'd said that, hadn't he?

"Almost there." Evangeline's voice radiated excitement.

They turned through the first doorway, which led into the dining room across from the parlor. They hadn't spent much time in the room. Instead, Spencer had always seemed more inclined to eat in the kitchen at the table there.

Spencer guided her into the room and then moved behind her, situating his hands on her hips. As his chest brushed up against her back, she almost allowed herself to sink into him. But she guessed Tex was still there too.

And of course Evangeline.

She had to wait until later to let her passion for him show.

He bent closer, his arms closing in from behind. A second later, his scruffy chin brushed her ear then her cheek, sending a shudder of pure pleasure through her. "Are you ready?" His voice echoed in her ear, and even that did strange things to her body.

"You do know that you don't have to do anything else." She turned to whisper. "Your love is all I need."

"Darling, this is only the first of many ways I plan to show you my love."

With that, he took a slight step back and loosened the blindfold. It fell away, and she found herself peering at a freshly painted dining room, the walls a lovely warm yellow. The dining room table still stood in the middle. But it was covered by a canvas, and a wooden turntable sat in the center containing jars that were filled with what appeared to be her supply of paintbrushes, pencils, calligraphy pens, measuring sticks, scissors, and more.

A large shelving unit lined the far wall. The wood was new, freshly constructed, and it hadn't been painted yet. Immediately her mind could picture it in a rich shade of lavender. It was lined with small storage boxes. Some seemed to hold more of her art supplies from the room upstairs. Many were still empty.

What could all of this mean?

Evangeline was clapping her hands and dancing in place. "What do you think of your new craft room, Mama?"

Patience drew in a sharp breath and brought both hands up to still her wildly beating heart. "This? Is my craft room?"

"Don't you just love it?" Evangeline spun in place, her eyes twinkling with her delight.

Patience could hardly take it all in, too overcome to believe that this was real and that she wasn't just dreaming.

Spencer was grinning, his slanted brows not so sad anymore but still just as appealing. "Open the trunks."

The two trunks from the back of the wagon now sat on the floor near the shelves.

Evangeline tugged her toward them and then proceeded to open the trunks for Patience. At the sight of mounds of additional craft supplies—everything she'd ever ordered at the store . . . and more—she cupped a hand over her mouth to hold back a cry of surprise.

Spencer had followed and was standing beside her. She turned to him, needing to understand what this was about and why he'd given her so much.

He smiled at her tenderly. "This is so that you can continue to fill our home with your beauty and life and creative touch. I need it, and so does Evangeline."

His words from the barn resounded in her head and

in her heart, when he'd told her the very same thing. And now, here he was proving it by giving her everything she needed to keep doing her projects. He not only loved her *in spite of* her messes—he loved her *because of* them.

She didn't know how to communicate to him just how much she'd needed to know that and how much it meant. It would take much more than an average thank-you to express it. It would take a kiss.

She took a step nearer, her gaze fixed on his lips.

His dropped to hers, sending spirals of need tightening inside her.

Just as she emboldened herself once again to initiate a kiss, Evangeline's excited chatter brought her back to reality. The child was taking out the items in the first chest and spreading them out on the floor in display— bright paper, new paints, bottles of glue, even the colored pencils she'd wanted but hadn't yet gotten.

Evangeline.

Patience tore her sights away from Spencer and fixed them on the girl.

"Evangeline, darling." Spencer was exchanging a look with Tex. "I have a surprise for you out in the barn."

She jumped up immediately. "What is it, Papa?"

He chuckled and mussed her hair. "You'll have to go with Tex and see."

She skipped through the dining room to where Tex stood in the doorway. She paused and looked back at them. "Aren't you coming?"

"I have something I need to tell your mama first."

That seemed to satisfy the child, and she finished skipping out of the room. Tex paused and winked at them, a grin splitting his face. "I'll keep her for a bit so that you can do all the *telling* you want."

Spencer grinned back.

As soon as the front door closed behind them, he lifted his hand and caressed Patience's cheek.

The touch was so feathery and fine that she wanted to lean into him and give him permission to continue. But now that they were alone again, she couldn't keep her nervousness from rushing back. "That was kind of you to have a surprise for Evangeline too."

"The new saddle for her pony arrived yesterday."

"She'll be excited."

He caressed her other cheek. "Yes, but I admit I saved it for this morning because I wanted to have you alone and all to myself for a few minutes."

"You did?"

"I figured that I might need to do a little more convincing at this point." When his gaze dropped to her mouth, she finally caught on to what he'd done by sending Evangeline away, and she smiled.

"That's good." She let her gaze settle on his lips too, the flames flaring and licking her insides. "Because I think I'm needing quite a bit of convincing at this moment."

He bent in and gave her the kiss she'd been wishing for since his last one. A kiss that held the promise of many more just like it.

Author's Note

Dear Readers, thank you for your enthusiasm over my Colorado Cowgirl series and for coming along for another ride, this time for Patience's story in *Convincing the Cowgirl*.

Again, I want to take a quick minute to thank all the people involved in getting my books—specifically *this* book—ready for publication. At the top of the list is my fabulous assistant, Rel Mollet. I'm eternally grateful for all your help!

I also couldn't produce such excellent books without the help of my editor Katie Donovan. And I'm super grateful for the amazing talent of Roseanna White for my covers.

A huge thank you to all my beta readers who are on my First Reader team! I so appreciate all of your keen eyes in catching my typos. Special thanks for this book to Zanese, Edward, Gina, Katie, and Natalie.

A big thank you to all my Review Crew members as

well. I love all of your enthusiasm and appreciate all of your reviews! Having your support and seeing your excitement is truly one of the highlights of being an author.

Finally, thank you, Readers, for all your support and encouragement. You are the best! If you want to stay up-to-date on all my book news, then visit me at jodyhedlund.com. Or join my Facebook Reader Room at facebook.com/groups/jodyhedlundsreaderroom

Jody Hedlund is the bestselling author of more than forty novels and is the winner of numerous awards. Jody lives in Michigan with her husband, busy family, and five spoiled cats. She writes sweet historical romances with plenty of sizzle.

A complete list of my novels can be found at jodyhedlund.com.

Would you like to know when my next book is available? You can sign up for my newsletter, become my friend on Goodreads, like me on Facebook, or follow me on Twitter.

Newsletter: jodyhedlund.com
Facebook: AuthorJodyHedlund
Twitter: @JodyHedlund

The more reviews a book has, the more likely other readers are to find it. If you have a minute, please leave a rating or review. I appreciate all reviews, whether positive or negative.